THE WITCH WHO KNEW THE GAME

PIXIE POINT BAY BOOK 4

EMMA BELMONT

EMMA ONLINE

Emma loves hearing from her readers!

You can contact her at the links below.

Website: emmabelmont.com

Newsletter: emmabelmont.com/newsletter

Thanks!

1

Maris Seaver couldn't remember the last time that dinner had been served at the Bed and Breakfast. But as she sat at the dining room table with Cookie and the B&B's four guests, she had to wonder if it wouldn't be a fun thing to do from time to time. Of course, since Cookie didn't regularly prepare lunch or dinner, it'd have to be done as it was being done tonight.

"For our first course," Etienne Fournier said, bringing the small white plate to Maris's place mat, "a salmon canapé."

The owner of Plateau 7, the five-star restaurant on the bay, was dressed in the traditional chef's uniform and hat. In his early sixties, he was of medium height with dark hair and flinty black eyes, and a pointed mustache that was waxed to a precise perfection.

"Local salmon on a fresh cucumber slice," he continued, with a slight French accent, setting the next plate in front of Cookie. "Finished with a lemon truffle mayonnaise."

"Beautiful," she said. Ruth "Cookie" Calderon, the B&B's diminutive older chef, smiled up at him, her dark eyes shining. "It's very good of you to leave the restaurant during the dinner hour."

As a fellow professional, she had appreciated the meaning of his presence. But Maris paused for a moment, regarding the man. Had Cookie not mentioned his restaurant, it wouldn't have occurred to her that Chef Fournier had left his business at its daily peak of customers. She gazed down at her canapé. This dinner must have come at quite the price tag.

Fournier smiled and inclined his head to the B&B's chef. "Thank you," he said. "But I am quite sure that the kitchen there is well taken care of."

The French chef moved on to serve the big man at the head of the table, Reggie Atkinson. A red-head with a matching red beard and hazel eyes, Reggie was the leader of the group. He'd reserved the entire B&B for the weekend and arranged for the catered dinner months ago. He called this get-together a "company off-site" for the key employees of his business: Whiz Kid Games.

"Bon appétit," the chef bid them.

Reggie smiled down at the little morsel, and then at each member of his group. "Let's start."

"This looks amazing," Pammy said, reaching for it. But when the Filipino man next to her picked up his fork, she paused. Then she picked up hers.

Blonde, blue-eyed, and more than a touch on the nerdy side, Pammy wore glasses that were round, thick, and framed in black. Maris had already noted that Pammy and the man next to her were pals. He waited for her to spear the appetizer and then they tasted it together. Her eyes widened as she made an appreciative sound, and nodded.

Like Pammy, Felix was in his early thirties. But unlike her or the rest of the group, he was easily the least nerdy, with his spiked hair and artsy goatee.

His dark eyes lit up as he enjoyed the

canapé. He brought a napkin to his mouth. "I like this," he said, reaching for his glass of white wine. "A lot."

Reggie had used his big fingers and simply popped the cucumber and salmon in his mouth. He nodded, still chewing. "Very nice," he said. "What do you think, BJ?"

The final member of the group had used a knife to cut his in half and had finished the first section. He'd just been about to eat the second piece, but paused. "I'm savoring it," he said with an enormous smile. "Because I'd eat this all evening if I could."

BJ sat opposite Pammy and was either the nerdiest of the group or the most avant-garde. Probably in his mid-forties, his dark hair had gone prematurely gray and he wore it cropped close. But it was his enormous fluorescent green glasses that made him stand out. They were so bright that they cast a slightly greenish hue to his brown eyes.

Maris decided to cut her appetizer in half as well. Sometimes the second bite could reveal the more complex flavors in a dish. The first bite, however, was divine. The brined salmon melted in her mouth, and the cucumber had a fresh and crisp texture that was the perfect compliment to it. The lemon truffle mayo left a nice lingering aftertaste that did indeed leave her wanting more.

Cookie nodded. "Perfect," was all she said.

The French chef inclined his head toward her, his mustache lifting at the sides, though he said nothing. He glanced around the table, and began to remove the plates.

Maris turned to Reggie, who was finishing a sip of wine. "Are you planning on seeing some of Pixie Point Bay's local sites while you're here?"

"Oh, absolutely," the big man said, his equally big voice rumbling. "It's finally a chance for us all to unwind a bit."

"I'm looking forward to seeing the redwoods for the first time," BJ said. His broad smile lifted his bright green glasses.

"I'm going to do something out on the bay," Pammy said, watching the chef set a bowl down in front of her. "Oh, this looks *wonderful*."

"French onion soup," he said. "Sweet onions in vegetable stock with white wine, seasoned with garlic, thyme, and pepper." He set the next bowl down in front of Felix.

"Topped with Gruyere and Swiss cheese, of course." He went back to the tray on the sideboard.

"Felix," Maris said to him, "are you planning on getting out?"

He laughed a little as he picked up his spoon. "I don't know. I'm not sure I remember what that's like."

"Oh my god, is that the sun?" Pammy joked as she pretended to squint.

"Look, the sky," BJ chimed in. "It's still blue."

As Maris was served her soup, she took in the savory aroma. The cheese spilled artfully over the edges of the small white bowl and not only looked melted but also slightly toasted in spots. With a supreme exercise of willpower, she tore her eyes from it and looked around the table. "I take it you all work long hours?"

There was laughter again, just as the last soup was served to Reggie, who said, "That smells amazing." Without a moment of hesitation, he dug in. Everyone else did likewise.

Maris tasted a bit of the broth first, and her appreciative "Mmm" joined those of the others. For a few minutes, there was only the sound of happy diners. A seemingly simple dish, the hot soup struck just the right balance between the savory onion and the salty but creamy cheese.

"I've changed my mind," BJ announced. "Now I want *this* for the rest of the evening."

Everyone laughed a little, too busy eating to make more jokes.

But eventually Reggie answered Maris's question. "We put in some crazy long hours," he said, "all of us, and this is a well-deserved getaway."

"Thank you, again, Reggie," Pammy said, her eyes big and expressive inside the round lenses.

Next to her, Felix nodded. "Yes, thank you." Pammy elbowed him and indicated his goatee, where a small string of cheese clung. He took his napkin from his lap and quickly wiped it. She nodded.

Conversation turned to the lighthouse, and Maris filled them in on its Victorian heritage, with the conical white tower being built first, in 1885. Then the lightkeeper's house, today's B&B, following a few years after that. But as Etienne cleared away the soup bowls, Maris was more curious about what the group did than the history of her home.

"I take it that Whiz Kid Games makes games?" she said.

"So to speak," Reggie said. "Actually, we're a publisher."

She cocked her head at him, but before she could ask him what a game publisher did, Etienne reappeared with the main course: crab legs, colossal ones, too big to fit on one of the B&B's standard plates. But he'd brought his own. If Maris had to guess, each long leg was more than a pound. Appreciative murmurs and a low whistle went up from around the table.

"Fresh caught Dungeness crab," he said, putting the first of the three plates he carried in front of Reggie, "served with cheese-and-potato pancakes and steamed baby carrots." He set the next enormous plate in front of BJ. "Also on the side are local organic greens topped with an aged balsamic vinaigrette." He set the third plate in front of Pammy and headed back to the kitchen.

The room seemed to settle into a stunned awe, all eyes on the plates. But eventually Cookie took a sip of water.

"So you publish games," she said, putting the glass down, "not create them?"

Reggie had been staring at his plate, but looked up at her with a broad smile. "We do a bit of both." He glanced at the sideboard, to a small stack of pamphlets that Maris hadn't previously noticed. "In fact," he said, "it's easier to demonstrate than explain."

He pushed his chair back from the table, fetched the pamphlets, and returned to his seat. Though Reggie was grinning, BJ, Pammy, and Felix were all staring at the pamphlets with stunned looks. Chef Fournier returned with the remaining plates and served them—in total silence. Although everyone had their dinner, no one moved to eat.

"You have got to be kidding," BJ said, glaring at Reggie. His fingers clutched the stem of his wine glass so hard that his knuckles had gone white and glossy. For a moment Maris worried he might snap it.

Reggie ignored him and focused on Cookie. "You'll be fascinated to know that our upcoming publication is a murder mystery dinner." He handed two pamphlets to Cookie, and she passed one to Maris. He arched his eyebrows at Maris. "And it just happens to take place at a Victorian B&B."

"No," Pammy muttered and sat back.

Felix moaned and put his head in his hands. "I should have known," he muttered.

Maris exchanged an alarmed look with Cookie. The convivial five course meal had just devolved into something else.

Reggie opened his pamphlet. "Shall we?"

2

———

Maris looked at the booklet titled "Betrayal at the Bed and Breakfast." On the upper half was a small Victorian home that looked like it was in an English village. On the bottom half was a drawing of a chalk outline around a body. At the very bottom was the Whiz Kid Games logo of electrons whirling around a nucleus with a byline crediting B.J. Ridder.

"This is lovely," Maris said, still gazing at it.

"Thanks," Pammy muttered.

Maris looked up at her. "Are you the illustrator?"

"Artist and art director," she replied, sullenly.

Etienne returned with the plates for the

shells and set them down. "Everyone has a crab cracker and fork." He paused and cast a glance at the stack of pamphlets next to Reggie. "Lemon and clarified butter are here." He indicated a sauce boat and a bowl of lemon wedges. "But please, taste it without first. I think you will be pleasantly surprised." When no one began eating, he scowled. Under his sizeable nose, the perfect mustache twitched back and forth and, if Maris wasn't mistaken, his ears were turning red. Now he glared at each of the diners and then the pamphlets.

Cookie set the paper down and picked up a crab leg and cracker. "This looks lovely, Chef."

"Bon," he said, before giving her a curt nod. Then he turned on his heel and left.

Cookie gave Maris a pained look, prompting her to set her pamphlet down as well. As she picked up one of the three large crab legs from her plate, she was astonished to find it was still warm. But the crab cracker was barely big enough to fit around the shell. As she squeezed, it occurred to her how big the crab must have been. Finally the shell gave way with a splintering sound, and the sweet and briny scent of the meat filled her nostrils.

As she reached for a lemon wedge she said, "BJ, I see your name is on the cover of the game book. Did you write 'Betrayal at the Bed and Breakfast'?"

He was using his fork to cut into the cheesy potato pancakes. "Yes," was all he said, glaring at his plate.

"BJ is our game designer," Reggie said, smiling as he cracked a crab leg. He broke it open and then used the tiny fork to tease out a good chunk of white meat. "We've been working together since college." He popped the crab in his mouth. "Mmm," he sighed as he closed his eyes.

Felix had picked up a crab leg, but dropped it back on his plate with a loud thunk. "Look," he said, glaring at Reggie, "this is supposed to be a vacation. A weekend off."

Pammy looked up from her plate and nodded. "Exactly."

"Honestly, Reg," BJ said, "this is pretty lame."

In the sudden silence, the sound of Cookie cracking a crab leg was incredibly loud. When she winced, Maris gave her a sympathetic look.

Reggie finished his first bite of crab. "Listen to you people," he admonished them. "You'd think we were at the office with stale pizza." He gestured to the table. "Instead we're eating a five course meal from a five-star restaurant." He pointedly looked at Felix's plate. "Which is getting cold, by the way."

"How could you bring the game?" Pammy asked, a slight whine to her voice. "It's the last thing any of us want to see."

"We won't need to see it for much longer," Reggie said. He paused for a dramatic moment. "I've sold the game to Hario."

BJ put down his fork and gaped at him. "*You what?*"

Reggie smiled at him. "We're not going to publish it. They are."

Felix and Pammy exchanged a quick look that Maris couldn't quite read. Surprise? Guarded pleasure?

The artist looked at Reggie, her blue eyes big behind the round lenses. "Then we don't need to play test it."

Reggie smiled beneficently at her, as

though she was a child. "We've got to dot the i's and cross the t's. It's a two-hour play test, tops. Then we have the rest of the weekend. We don't even have to start at the beginning."

"Of course you do," Felix said, picking up the crab leg again. "It's a murder mystery."

BJ and Pammy both shot a glare at him, but he just shrugged in reply.

"And where better to do it?" Reggie asked, still smiling. "In a beautiful locale, in an actual Victorian B&B." He gestured around with his fork. "It doesn't get any better." He shoveled some cheesy potato pancake into his mouth.

Pammy picked at her carrots. "It's like bait and switch," she muttered.

The group sank into another silence, but Reggie continued to relish his dinner. Although BJ and Felix began to crack crab legs, Maris wondered how they'd manage to eat with tight jaws and deep frowns. Rather than discuss the game, she decided to take a different tack.

As she squeezed some lemon onto her crab meat, she said, "I only learned recently that Chef Fournier was an instructor at Le Cordon Bleu. His restaurant, Plateau 7, is the only restaurant in Pixie Point Bay with an ocean view."

"Cordon Bleu?" Pammy said quietly and seemed to take a new interest in her plate.

Felix glanced toward the dark bay window. "The *only* one with a view?" he asked. "Why is that?"

"It's a simple matter of geography," Cookie said as she speared some of the greens. "Most of the coast is too rocky, or the beaches too narrow, or the cliffs too steep."

"There are only three establishments on the bay itself," Maris said. "The pier, Plateau 7, and our lighthouse."

Felix's eyebrows rose. "Some pretty pricey property I imagine."

"The lighthouse and attached lightkeeper's house have been in my family since the late 1800s," Maris said, smiling. "I'm afraid I don't keep up with real estate prices."

BJ smirked at her as he poured clarified butter over everything on his plate. "Pretty pricey property."

At that moment, Chef Fournier returned with a cheese tray, but seeing that no one had yet finished the main course, he frowned and set it on the sideboard.

"Chef," Maris said to him. "I have never tasted such sweet and tender crab meat."

Pammy turned around. "These cheesy potato pancakes are to die for," she gushed.

Felix nodded, covering his mouth with his hand. "Best potatoes I've ever had."

The chef gave them a stiff little bow. "Thank you," he said, managing to smile.

Maris noted that Reggie didn't join in the conversation. Although he'd clearly been enjoying his meal—his plate was clean—he'd let the others talk or ask questions. But now he turned to the chef as well.

"Maris tells us you taught at Le Cordon Bleu," Reggie said, smiling. "In Paris?"

The chef quickly shook his head. "No, no, no. I *trained* in Paris. I taught in Sydney, Australia."

"Another oceanside town," Felix noted.

Fournier inclined his head. "Just as you say. Sydney is where my love affair with fresh seafood began."

Maris had to smile. The chef's romance with seafood was clearly evident.

"Is the fresh catch much different than what's available here?" Cookie asked.

"Oh very," he said, clasping his hands together. "The fresh prawns and oysters of Sydney are unlike any others." His dark eyes sparkled. "And the Tasmanian Ocean Trout?" He gave two emphatic okay signs. "Less salty and much more subtle than salmon." He rolled his eyes. "But the same beautiful texture and color." Although he looked as though he'd go on, he noticed Reggie's empty plate. "May I?" he asked, indicating it.

"Yes," the big man said. "I don't think I have ever enjoyed a meal so much."

"Thank you," Fournier said. He turned to BJ, indicating the plate, and the game developer nodded. "That was excellent."

The chef inclined his head, picked up his plate, and took both to the sideboard. Then he returned with the cheese tray. "Local and farm fresh from Cheeseman Village we have a feta, a truffle Gouda, a Parmesan, and the Village's version of Gorgonzola."

"I love cheese for dessert," Reggie said, reaching for the Gouda.

"No, no, no," Etienne said, as he picked up Cookie's plate. "This is not dessert. This evening we finish with an almond tart."

Cookie smiled up at him. "The quintessential French classic."

He grinned, lifting the sharp points of his mustache. "Precisely." He gestured to Maris's plate. "May I?"

Maris nodded. "I think you'd better if there's an almond tart coming." There was light laughter around the table, but she saw Reggie glancing at his murder mystery pamphlet. Rather than let him ruin the nice mood, she picked up her own game booklet, regarded it and then Reggie.

"Earlier you referred to a play test," she said. "What exactly is that?"

Although BJ grimaced, Pammy only sighed and Felix reached for a piece of Parmesan. The chef took the tray of dishes from the room.

"It's the last phase of production before a game is released," Reggie told her. "Sometimes we send it out to play testers in the gaming community. They get a free game and we get honest feedback."

"Back when we were really part of the community," BJ said, cocking an eyebrow at Reggie.

"But since we're here," Reggie said, ignoring him, "in the most perfect of locations, we can play test it ourselves, and have it done."

Maris noted the return of the sour looks across the table. She exchanged a look with Cookie, who nodded, before Maris glanced down at the game book.

"If it'd help," Maris said, "Cookie and I can play."

Felix looked up from his cheese. "It actually might."

Pammy looked at Cookie and Maris. "Have you ever played a murder mystery game before?"

They shook their heads. "I'm afraid not," Maris said. "I've never even seen one before."

"Then that's perfect," Reggie said.

Etienne returned with a tray of six fluted white ramekins filled with golden brown pastries dusted with almond slivers and powdered sugar. "Tarte aux Amandes," he announced. The delicate aroma of the sweet almonds filled the room.

"Dessert first," Reggie said, beaming at the chef, "play test second."

3

———————

Maris carried the last of the insulated bags back to the Plateau 7 minivan. Etienne loaded the plastic storage box that held some of his tools into the back seat. As he took the carry bag from her, he said, "Thank you."

He'd been upset ever since the appearance of the game pamphlets, and Maris could hardly blame him. The five course meal had not been easy to prepare or serve. After twenty-five years in the hospitality trade, Maris knew that the timing of meal service could be critical to the food's temperature, texture, and even the flavor—and hence the enjoyment. The chef had adjusted magnificently, and the food had been amazing, but

Maris knew he must have felt that the focus on the meal had been hijacked.

He took off his chef's hat and threw it down on the storage box with a sound of disgust. Then he slammed the sliding door of the van closed.

"Impossible," he muttered. "They should have ordered burgers."

She gave him an understanding smile. "I've never been treated to such a magnificent meal in my own B&B," Maris told him. She quickly recounted the beautifully portioned canapé, the perfectly melted cheese over the flavorful onion soup, and the sweet and tender meat of the largest crab legs she'd ever had the pleasure to meet. With each description of the five courses, the chef seemed to relax a bit. By the time she got to the artful almond tart and how she hoped its fragrance would linger in the dining room all night, he seemed mildly pleased and somewhat placated.

"Truly," she finished. "A masterpiece."

"Well," he sniffed, glancing back at the front door. "I am gratified that someone enjoyed it."

Maris laughed a little. "Oh more than that, Chef, and more than me, I assure you."

He hesitated a moment before he asked, "And Cookie, do you think she approved?"

Maris smiled to herself. Of course the chef would be most interested in what another chef thought. She nodded. "I have never seen her eat more at one sitting. She said more than once that the food was *amazing*."

He put a hand to his heart. "Oh, I am...so relieved." He glanced at the front door again. "Bon."

As he climbed into his van, Maris waited and, as he pulled away, gave him a good-bye wave. She had to smile at the thought that an instructor for Le Cordon Bleu would be worried about what the B&B's chef thought. It was more than professional courtesy. To be fair, though, Cookie's breakfasts outshone anything Maris had ever encountered in any hotel. The French chef's concern was well founded.

Maris went back into the B&B and was pleased to find that the Whiz Kid group and Cookie had moved to the living room. Reggie was explaining the rules.

He handed Maris a pamphlet as she entered. "You'll be the B&B owner, a kindly Victorian widow trying to make ends meet by renting out rooms."

"Mrs. Winter," Maris read from the cover and opened it. "You are–"

"Don't tell anybody about your character," Reggie quickly interjected. "That information is just for you."

"Oh," Maris said. She looked around at everyone else's pamphlet. Each had a different character name. "Okay."

"Cookie will be the widow's spinster cousin," Reggie said, nodding to her. "Felix is the traveling salesman. Pammy is a lady of the night. BJ is the permanent boarder who works as a local carpenter." Reggie showed her his pamphlet. "Mr. Orange is a gambler."

BJ snorted. "No surprise there." Although Reggie glared at him, the game designer glared right back.

Cookie had been studying her character information but looked up. "I see this takes place in Victorian England. Would your game players wear period clothing?"

Reggie nodded. "That's part of the allure.

They make dinner too, and sometimes try to be true to the period with the meals as well. The kit comes with invitations, recommendations for the costumes, and a background story."

Maris scanned the information about her character. As Reggie had said, the B&B owner was recently widowed, with no children. But with no work skills and a new mortgage that needed paying, Mrs. Winter has had to take on boarders and guests in order to keep from going to the poor house. It's a tremendous amount of work, not made any easier by the presence of her spinster cousin, who doesn't do anything to help.

Maris looked up from her pamphlet. "Does anyone know who the murderer is?"

"None of the players do except the host," Reggie answered. "But of course, as the publishers, we know."

Which is why, Maris supposed, that BJ had said it'd be perfect that neither Maris nor Cookie had played one of these games before. But as she glanced around the room, she saw the other members of Whiz Kid Games were decidedly uninterested. BJ had been looking at his phone the entire time since she'd returned. Felix and Pammy hadn't seemed to hear anything that had been said, since they'd been whispering to each other non-stop.

Reggie cleared his throat. "Shall we begin?" He turned to Maris. "I believe the action begins with Mrs. Winter pouring wine for everyone after dinner."

"Oh?" Maris said, looking at her pamphlet. "Yes, I see." She looked around at the group, settling on Reggie. "And is that what I should do?"

"I could use a glass of wine," Felix said.

"If you don't mind," Pammy added.

Maris smiled at the group. "It's a normal part of the B&B's evening actually."

While Maris poured and served the wine, Reggie gave the other character's their directions. For the next hour or so, they moved from room to room, sometimes together and other times alone, acting out their parts in the living room, the library, the parlor, and the dining room. Apparently the bed and breakfast served dinner and all of the characters had gathered for the meal at the end of the day.

While some knew each other, the rest had to introduce themselves. Maris and Cookie tried to be careful only to reveal what their booklets said could be revealed. A bored Pammy had her woman of the evening spend most of her time with Reggie, the gambler. Felix's traveling salesman tried to sell Cookie's character some gloves, while the permanent boarder that BJ played stayed in the kitchen waiting for the meal.

But at one point, Maris ended up with Cookie in the parlor.

"You're doing very well," Maris told her.

Cookie stooped and held her aching back. "You young people," she said, making her voice tremble. "Always expecting too much from your elders."

"Well, maybe *you'd* like to pay the mortgage," Maris said sternly. "Then I could hire a housekeeper."

The two of them laughed, until they heard Pammy yell, "*He's dead.*"

Maris and Cookie exchanged an alarmed look and ran toward Pammy's voice in the library. Although Reggie was lying on the floor, he raised his head and looked at everyone. "So far so good," he said. Then he grunted as he sat up, grabbed his nearby wine glass, and took a swig. He seemed about to say something, when a tiny, tinny harmonica-like meow drew everyone's attention to the door.

"Who is this?" Pammy exclaimed, as Mojo trotted over to Reggie.

The big man lifted his glass out of the way. "Well, hello there." The little black cat climbed into his sizeable lap.

"This would be Mojo," Cookie said, in her tremulous voice.

Pammy grinned at her. "What a perfect name for him." She crouched down and gave his head a little scratch. "His eyes are gorgeous."

Reggie stroked Mojo's back and then took a sip of his wine. "Okay, so now the gambler is dead."

Maris cocked her head at him. "But what do you do now? Do you have to lay there for the rest of the evening?"

Reggie grinned at her. "Not at all," he said, continuing to stroke the back of a supremely satisfied looking cat. "Now I'm the ghost of the gambler. I'm not allowed to speak with you but I can–" The big man stopped, held his stomach, and hiccuped. "Scuse me," he said, slurring a little. Then he hiccuped again.

"Try holding your breath," BJ said.

But when Reggie tried, only to hiccup again, Felix said under his breath, "Try drinking less."

Reggie moved Mojo off his lap, as he hiccuped yet again. "Here," he said, giving his wine glass to Pammy. "Could you hold that for a second?"

He struggled to get up, but BJ finally held out a hand and—with some effort—tugged him up. Though the big man tottered for a moment, he managed to stand. He held out his hand for his wine glass, but Pammy hesitated. She looked at BJ and Felix.

"Oh come on," Reggie said, just before he hiccuped so loud he surprised himself.

"Okay," Felix said. "That's it. I didn't come here to work, and I certainly didn't come here to play test with someone who's drunk." He dropped his booklet on the coffee table and picked up his own wine glass. "Thank you," he said to Maris and Cookie. "Both for the wine and for your patience."

Reggie scowled at him. "They're having a good time and I'm not drunk."

Pammy handed him back his glass. "I'm going to bed." She turned to Maris and Cookie and added, "Good night." Then she put her pamphlet with the others and followed Felix up the stairs.

"Good night," Cookie replied.

"Sleep well," Maris said.

Then she and Cookie exchanged a look and the B&B's chef shrugged, placed her booklet on the pile, and picked up Pammy's empty wine glass. She took it to the kitchen.

"Oh come on," Reggie groaned. "It'll only take...like half an hour. And I stopped hiccuping!" But the last phrase was slurred.

"This was a bad idea from the start," BJ said to him, pushing his bright green glasses up his nose. Then he headed after Felix and Pammy. "I'll see you in the morning."

In just moments it was only Reggie and Maris in the library. He looked at her. "Well, Mrs. Winter, I'm afraid the mystery of the Betrayal at the Bed and Breakfast is over." He paused, looked at his wine glass, and then back at her. He glanced at the stairs as though he might call the group back. Then he shrugged. "Oh well." He lifted his still half-full wine glass to her. "Thank you for a lovely evening, and..." He paused to grab the game books from the table. "For at least trying the game."

"My pleasure, Reggie," she said, giving him her booklet. "It was interesting and entertaining—and thank you for dinner."

He nodded to her before he weaved his way over to the stairs. As Maris followed behind at a discreet distance, she watched him go up the steps, and waited. When she heard the door to his room close, she sighed with a bit of relief and turned away.

In the kitchen, Maris found Cookie loading the glasses into the dishwasher. The diminutive chef looked up at her, smiling. "That was fun."

Maris grinned back. "I didn't know you were such an actress."

"Me either," Cookie said chuckling. She closed the dishwasher. "But I guess I'm not a natural, because now I am just plain worn out."

Maris nodded as they headed to the hallway, and Cookie turned off the kitchen light. At the end of the hall, they parted company.

Maris peeked into her room and saw that Mojo had already found his place on the bed. Then she poked her head back out into the hallway. "Sleep well, Cookie."

"Sweet dreams," Cookie said, and they both closed their doors.

4

In the morning, Maris and Mojo found the previous evening's aroma of almond tart replaced with the scrumptious smell of Cookie's breakfast. As soon as she opened her bedroom door, Mojo trotted down the hall toward the kitchen—and Maris could hardly blame him. Not only had the B&B acquired a reputation for its beautiful location, Cookie's breakfasts were becoming legendary.

As usual, Cookie stood at the stove, her back to the door. But as Maris entered, she glanced over her shoulder, smiling. "Good morning."

"Good morning," Maris said with her usual cheer.

For decades in the hospitality trade,

Maris had known she was a morning person. Eager to get up and start the day, it didn't matter if the sun was up yet or not. Whatever cares the previous night had carried, the morning always seemed to ease them. But as Maris looked at Cookie smiling down at her skillets, she realized that the older woman was always happy in the morning too. But Maris guessed it was more to do with the cooking than simply the start of the day. As far as she could remember, Cookie was happy at the stove.

Maris peeked over her shoulder. "Breakfast Quesadillas," she murmured. "My favorite."

Cookie grinned at her but drew her brows together. "I thought the Breakfast Pie was your favorite."

"When there's Breakfast Pie, it's my favorite." She eyed the skillet. "When there's Breakfast Quesadillas, they're my favorite. I'm very...*egalitarian* that way."

Not only did the quesadillas have the fluffy scrambled eggs that Cookie was known for, but green peppers, local lox, and fresh jack and cheddar cheeses from Cheeseman Village. The quesadillas were cooked until the cheese was melted and the tortillas had turned a golden brown. Then they were folded over the already cooked contents that had been ladled onto one side of the tortilla. Once folded, Cookie expertly moved it to the warming tray and started the next.

Hash browns were cooking in another large iron skillet, and Maris saw that assorted Danish waited on the counter, along with fresh cantaloupe and mangos.

She had just been about to ask what she could do to help, when a harmonica-like meow drew her attention to the floor. Mojo sat next to his empty bowl in the corner near the dishwasher, staring at her with his big orange eyes. He meowed again, plaintively this time.

"You'd think I never feed you," Maris said, heading to the oversized stainless refrigerator. She removed the plastic container with his food, the only thing he would eat: smoked salmon. There'd been a couple of times she was tempted to eat it herself. But instead, she forked some of the flaky fish into his bowl and watched as he dove at it face first. "Um, bon appétit."

As Cookie transferred the hash browns to

a warming tray, she said, "Speaking of which, Chef Fournier put on quite the meal."

Maris nodded as she put away the salmon. "Beautifully prepared and served," she said, and then raised an eyebrow at the cook. "But really, I think it saved the evening." She picked up the warming tray full of quesadillas. "Be right back."

At the dining room sideboard, Maris checked that the tray was plugged in and that the hot water dispenser was ready, before returning to the kitchen.

"I think you're right," Cookie said, as Maris picked up the hash browns. "You and I were the only ones interested in the game." She began to slice the cantaloupe.

"And Reggie," Maris noted, taking the hash browns out.

When she returned, Cookie was working on the mangos, so Maris started the coffee, got out the juicer, and began to peel oranges. After another several minutes, everything was ready. Cookie took the fresh fruit to the dining room, followed by the Danish, as Maris poured the juice into its pretty glass pitcher and the coffee into its vacuum sealed carafe. Only one thing remained—their tea.

Cookie returned for the infusers, which she'd already prepared. "Shall we?" she said.

As was the tradition at the Pixie Point Bay B&B, the chef and owner dined with the guests. Nor did they have long to wait. Felix and Pammy had apparently smelled the quesadillas. When they appeared at the door, Felix asked, "What smells so incredible?"

As he went to the sideboard, Pammy looked at Maris and Cookie. "I didn't think I could be hungry again after last night's meal, but..." She glanced at the warming trays.

"Good morning," Maris said smiling at them both. "That would be Cookie's world famous breakfast quesadillas that you smell."

"Breakfast quesadillas," Felix said to Pammy. "Look at this." Quickly he turned to Maris and Cookie, his smile beaming. "And good morning."

"Good morning," Pammy said as well.

Once the guests and Cookie had their food, Maris served herself a quesadilla, as well as a good helping of the fresh fruit. Though she looked at the different Danish rolls, she managed to stop herself from taking one. In her ongoing battle to lower her cholesterol and weight, she'd managed to make a little progress since returning to Pixie Point Bay. Now was the time to make more headway, not backtrack.

Once they were all settled, Maris thought back on the previous evening. "Felix," she said, "I don't think I heard what it is that you do at Whiz Kid Games."

He swallowed and wiped his mouth with a napkin. "I do what everybody else doesn't," he said, laughing a little. "My real title is producer. But I work on contracts, sourcing outside talent, budget, schedule, fact-checking, research... You know, pretty much anything but design." He used his fork and knife to slice through the quesadilla. "This is the best quesadilla I have ever had. Breakfast, lunch, or dinner."

"I'm glad you like it," Cookie said, and sipped her tea.

"We have salsa," Maris said, "if you'd like."

He shook his head. "It's perfect as is." Then he took another big bite.

"Have you both been in the gaming business for a while?" Maris asked them, spearing a piece of cantaloupe.

"Oh no," Pammy said, shaking her head.

"I did story boards for Paramount for about three minutes. I also drew my own graphic novel. Then I did product photography for an online hardware store." She shrugged and picked up her coffee. "Really, as an artist, you take what you can get." She took a sip.

"And you Felix?" Maris asked. "It seems you're a jack of all trades."

He nodded. "You've gotta be. But I've always been in the gaming industry." He grinned at her over a glass of orange juice. "One of the lucky few."

Maris smiled back, genuinely pleased for him. In her time in the hospitality industry, she'd run across many travelers of course, some of whom journeyed for the job. But it was the rare person who seemed to be doing the calling of their heart—like her.

"Are either of you planning anything in particular today?" Cookie asked, tea in hand.

Pammy adjusted her big round glasses and then glanced at the bay window. "Well, I'd hoped to do something out on that pretty bay, but with the fog, I don't know."

"It'll be gone my mid-morning," Maris assured her. "It always is." She nodded toward the back of the house. "We've got kayaks at the dock below the lighthouse."

"Really?" Pammy said, breaking apart her Danish. "I adore kayaking. That sounds like a winner."

"You know how to kayak?" Felix asked her.

Pammy nodded. "I've always been a water baby. The swim team in high school, water skiing at the old reservoir next to my parent's house, jet skiing in the ocean, canoes. Pretty much anything that has to do with the water. I love it all." She paused for a moment, then regarded him. "Do you want to learn how to kayak?"

He gulped his orange juice before he nodded vigorously. "Uh, yeah. That'd be great."

"The life vests and paddles are stowed inside," Maris told them.

"Life vests and paddles?" BJ said, appearing in the doorway. He put his hands on his hips. "Sounds like you're getting ready for one of our business meetings." His impish grin lifted the neon green glasses a little.

"Good morning," Maris said to him, as Pammy and Felix chuckled.

"Good morning," he replied, heading to the buffet. "I was going to sleep in, but my stomach said I'd better come down here and find out what was smelling so good."

"The breakfast quesadilla is awesome," Felix said.

By the time BJ got his plate and coffee, Cookie had finished and headed back to the kitchen. Maris, however, lingered over her tea.

"That was some stunt Reggie pulled last night," BJ said, lowering his voice.

Felix snorted, as he sat back. "It's the cash flow. He's really banking on this new game. I had no idea how tight the money was until he said he'd sold it."

BJ made a sour face. "That's for sure. I've been saying for months we needed something else in the pipeline."

"Well," Pammy said. "No matter what. It was nice of him to pay for this weekend." Almost as one, all three glanced to the second floor, as though Reggie were listening to them. "I'm surprised he hasn't come down yet."

BJ grimaced. "I'm not. He's probably embarrassed—as well he should be."

"Or hungover," Felix suggested.

Pammy looked at BJ. "We're going to go kayaking. Want to come along?"

BJ frowned as he looked at the two of them. "Can you get seasick on a kayak?"

"Honestly," Pammy said, "I don't know." She looked at Felix, who shrugged. Then she turned back to BJ. "Do you get seasick?"

BJ nodded as he chopped into some hash browns with the side of his fork. "At the drop of a hat really."

"There are lots of different things to do in the area that don't involve being on the ocean," Maris said. "I'd be glad to make some suggestions."

"That'd be great," BJ said. He glanced at the other two. "I'm afraid you guys are on your own."

Pammy and Felix left to go check out the kayaks and, while BJ enjoyed his breakfast, Maris described some of the different options: the redwoods, the dairy tour in Cheeseman Village, the wine tasting and flower farms down south, shopping in the Towne Plaza, and the tide pools north of the bay, to name but a few.

BJ finished the last of his juice. "The hikes

in the redwoods sound perfect. Not only do I feel the need to just get out in nature." He glanced down at his empty plate. "But I think I'd better work off some calories." He got up from the table. "Thanks very much for all the suggestions." He glanced up toward the second floor. "Guess I'll just get my jacket."

Maris took the plates and a couple of glasses to the kitchen, where Cookie was washing the iron skillets. As Maris set the plates on the counter to be rinsed, Cookie looked over at them.

"Not everyone had breakfast?" the chef asked.

Maris shook her head. "Reggie hasn't come down yet."

"Shall we leave the buffet out?"

Maris glanced back to the hallway. "Let's leave it for a little while more. If he doesn't come down soon, I'll save a plate for him."

5

While Cookie cleaned the bathrooms and made sure to provide fresh toiletries and towels, Maris turned down the beds and took away the trash. Although she would have liked to vacuum as well, Reggie's closed door stopped her. Rather than make noise, she would have to catch up with the vacuuming later.

As they made their way down the stairs, Maris said, "I think I'd better wait on the vacuuming downstairs too."

Cookie nodded. "Just to be safe." She glanced back up to the landing. "Maybe he's just a late night person."

Maris nodded. It was possible.

Sometimes the staff in hotels got worried

if the "Do Not Disturb" sign was left for more than a few days. But only rarely had it ever meant trouble. For the most part, Maris had found that people simply wanted their privacy. Once in a while there'd be a guest who worked a graveyard or swing shift. And of course at the casino resorts they gambled all night and then caught one of the midnight shows. In a few particularly torrid parts of the world, it only made sense to venture out once the sun went down. But finally there were those people whose natural rhythm was different than others. The first thing that Maris had done when the staff was worried was check room service. For the bigger properties with twenty-four hour kitchen staff, it was easy to spot the midnight owls. They'd order dinner at three in the morning.

Downstairs, Cookie started to launder the towels while Maris dusted the public rooms first. Although the Victorian decor was charming and beautiful, it took more care than a minimalist's dream. The antique wood had to be treated carefully, only dusted if possible, and then waxed if not. The intricate carvings and embellishments meant that even just dusting could be time consuming—

likewise the various Tiffany lamps, porcelain vases, and books. Even so, she and Cookie were pretty much done in under a few hours.

When they met outside the pantry, Cookie asked, "How about if I warm up the quesadilla leftovers for lunch?"

Often there were no leftovers. After decades of serving breakfast, Cookie could almost size up the guest's appetites. Since she ate with them, it was also a simple matter of watching the trays and making more if needed. She never cleaned the kitchen until the meal was over.

"Quesadillas would be wonderful," Maris said. "Thank you."

Then she looked up to the stairs, frowned, and crossed her arms. It'd be a good time to warm up Reggie's breakfast plate as well. Even if the company owner was a night owl, he'd said himself that the group would have the rest of the weekend for activities. Surely he'd included himself in that. Thinking back on the morning meal, the others had speculated that he might be embarrassed or hungover. There'd been no indication that sleeping late was his normal thing.

Cookie followed her gaze up the stairs. "Go ahead. He'll be glad for lunch."

Maris smiled at her. "True."

Outside Reggie's door, Maris tapped lightly. "Reggie?" She waited for several moments. Could he have left without her or Cookie noticing? She knocked a little more loudly. "Reggie?" she said. But again, she was met with silence. There hadn't even been the creaking of the bed. She knocked once more, with force. "Reggie, are you all right?"

Slowly, listening intently, she grasped the antique knob and turned it, opening the door just a crack. "Reggie?" she called inside. But as she slowly swung the door aside, she saw a large form in the bed under the comforter. "Oh, Reggie. I'm so sorry to disturb you." He was on his side and facing away from her. "Reggie?"

How could he not have heard her? She came around the foot of the bed, watching him. He hadn't moved an inch and she couldn't see if he was breathing. "Reggie," she said, as she came to the other side of the bed. "I've been–"

Though his eyes were closed and his hands were tucked under his head like a pillow, his skin had a bluish caste to it. "Reggie!" she exclaimed, shaking his shoulder. He wouldn't rouse. Quickly she put two fingers to his neck, and almost pulled them back. His skin was cold. Even as her stomach dropped like an elevator, she tried to find a pulse—to no avail.

"Oh, no," she muttered. She raced back to the door, dashed through it, and then hurried down the stairs. In the library she picked up the receiver of the antique phone and dialed the emergency number.

Cookie came out of the kitchen, wiping her hands on an apron. "What's the–"

When the emergency operator answered, Maris held up a finger to the chef. "Yes," she said into the receiver. "This is Maris Seaver at the Pixie Point Bay Lighthouse and B&B. I think one of my guests has died."

6

No sooner had the paramedic vehicle pulled up to the front of the B&B, than Mac's sheriff's SUV entered the long drive. Although Maris would have liked to wait for him, the two paramedics exited their vehicle with purpose, if not the headlong rush of trying to save someone's life. Even so, one of them carried a medical kit. The paramedic in front looked at her as he came up the steps of the porch.

"This way," she said, leading him through the open door.

Cookie was standing in the hallway, holding Mojo. "Oh, thanks, Cookie," Maris said, as they passed her. Mojo's glittering orange eyes seemed to watch them all. Though the little black cat had never expressed even the slightest interest in treading outside, she also didn't want him underfoot where he might get stepped on.

As she trotted up the stair steps, the big men behind her took them two at a time. She led them directly into Reggie's room and then stood back. The first man went directly to the body and felt the temperature of the forehead. The other opened the kit, took out a stethoscope, and placed it on the side of Reggie's neck.

Maris heard Mac's footsteps and turned to him as he entered. "Hello, Mac."

Sheriff Daniel "Mac" McKenna wore his usual brown and khaki uniform, with the six-pointed gold sheriff's badge above the breast pocket. The brightly colored patch on the long sleeve said "Medio County Sheriff." But he must have left the campaign hat in the vehicle.

He glanced quickly at the room and the paramedics before moving next to her.

"Maris," he said, touching her arm lightly. "I heard the emergency dispatch. Are you okay?"

In his early fifties, Mac was tall and well

built, with short salt and pepper hair. But his glittering gray eyes, normally smiling, were filled with worry as they met hers.

She tried to give him a smile. "Pretty good, considering someone has died in my home. You know."

He gave her a sympathetic look and gently rubbed her back between the shoulder blades. "Do you want to have a seat?"

She shook her head. "I had some water and sat down while I waited." She didn't mention that Cookie had made them both some tea. Because the chef's magical ability involved potions, it'd had both a soothing and restorative effect that she was doubly glad for now. "I'm fine, Mac, but thanks for asking."

"All right then." He took out a notepad from the breast pocket of his uniform shirt. "What can you tell me?"

But before she could start, the paramedic who'd felt Reggie's temperature said, "Sheriff, I think you'll want to have a look at this." He pointed at Reggie's face, which Maris could thankfully no longer see.

Mac went to the other side of the bed. His

eyebrows rose and he bent forward for a closer look.

"Could be poisoning," the paramedic said.

"Right," Mac muttered, straightening. He took the mobile phone from his utility belt and speed-dialed a number. "Hi, Genie, it's Mac. Get a forensics team and the coroner to the lighthouse in Pixie Point Bay ASAP, would you?" He listened for a moment. "Thanks." He hung up and put the phone back. As he fished a pair of latex gloves from his pants pocket, he said to Maris, "Tell me what you know."

As she recounted the evening, Mac carefully lifted the bedding and checked underneath. She told him about the other guests, the catered dinner, and the murder mystery game—and how unpopular it had been. As the paramedics began to pack up, he went to the dresser and picked up Reggie's empty wine glass. He sniffed it and frowned. Although the EMTs had been about to leave, he motioned the one with the kit over. He held the glass out.

"What do you smell?" the sheriff asked.

The big man sniffed and then wrinkled

his nose. "Bitters." He looked Mac in the eye. "Cyanide."

"That's what I was thinking," Mac said. He nodded to them both. "Thanks. There's no need for you to wait."

Maris put a hand to her pounding heart. Reggie had been poisoned? Mentally she ran through all the events of the previous evening—the ones she'd just explained to Mac. Reggie had acted drunk, not poisoned.

As the paramedics left, Mac put the wine glass back on the dresser.

"Let's talk outside," he said, gesturing for her to precede him. He closed the door behind him. "For now, that's a crime scene." He took off the gloves. "I'll probably be able to release the room once the forensics team is done and the coroner removes the body for an autopsy. Later today." He gestured to the stairs. "Let's find Cookie."

She was in the living room, but Mojo was nowhere to be seen. "I put him in your room," she said, seeing Maris look around. "He was tired of being held." She looked from Maris to the sheriff and back again. "What is it?"

"Reggie was poisoned," Maris said.

The diminutive chef cocked her head back and gaped at them. "What? Poisoned?"

Maris shook her head and moved to the nearest chair, sitting down hard. "I know. I can hardly believe it, let alone see how it could have been done."

"The wine glass is our best clue," Mac said. "But I'm afraid we can't assume that's it." They both looked at him. "I'm going to need any leftovers from the dinner, any wine bottles, empty or not, napkins, utensils, storage containers. Really, anything that might have come into contact with the food or drink."

"Almost everything was catered by Chef Fournier," Cookie said, standing. "But I'll go get the leftovers now. I'm afraid all the dishes have already been washed." She headed to the kitchen.

"I'll get the wine bottles," Maris said, standing. "The other glasses have been washed as well."

"Do you have any idea where the other guests have gone?"

Maris pointed toward the bay. "Pammy and Felix are out kayaking." Then she pointed inland. "BJ was going to hike in the redwoods."

"I don't suppose they said when they'd be returning?"

Maris shook her head. "I'm afraid not. Honestly, you just never know with guests. They might change their plans and stay out all day."

"Okay," Mac said, taking out his phone. "While we're waiting for the coroner and forensics, I'll call Plateau 7."

"I'll get those wine bottles."

7

As Cookie gathered together the few leftovers, mostly carrots and greens, Maris fetched what remained of the bottles of wine. But even as she did, she suspected there would be no evidence of poisoning in them. Everyone, including her, had sipped at least a little wine for the sake of the game. She could, of course, recall their movements during the evening, but the game had required them all to split up into different rooms at various points. All of the wine glasses had been left unattended at some point during the evening.

As Maris set the two bottles on the large butcher block in the kitchen along with the food, she heard a car pull up and the front door open. She peeked into the hallway and saw the forensics team arrive. Mac directed them upstairs and she went back into the kitchen. But then, not a minute later, the front door opened again.

"Are you a guest here?" she heard Mac ask.

Maris exited the kitchen to find that BJ had returned early from his day.

"Yes," BJ replied, frowning. He looked between them.

"Sheriff McKenna," Maris said, "this is BJ Ridder. BJ this is the sheriff of Medio County."

"What's going on?" the game developer asked.

"BJ," Maris said, gesturing to the living room. "Why don't you have a seat?"

Though he looked unsure, he followed her inside, followed by Mac. BJ took a seat as Maris did, while Mac stood near the door.

"BJ is staying here with the other Whiz Kid Games employees," she said.

Mac nodded. "I'm afraid I've got some bad news," he said. "Reginald Atkinson was found dead in his bed this afternoon."

BJ tilted his head sideways. "Reginald Atkinson?" He shook his head. "I don't understand. Are you talking about Reggie?" He looked at Maris, who gave him a slow nod as she grimaced. "Wait. What are you saying? Reggie is..." He gaped at Mac. "*Dead?*"

"Yes," the sheriff replied calmly. "His body was found earlier this afternoon by Maris."

"But...but," BJ stammered. His already pale skin seemed to go a shade lighter. "But how could that be?" His voice was a bit strident. "We were all together just last night." He was almost wailing now. "No." He shook his head. "It has to be a mistake."

Maris shook her head. "I'm so sorry, BJ, but there is no mistake. I'm afraid Reggie is dead."

The sound of a vehicle pulling up on the gravel drive outside the front window drew Mac's attention. "The coroner is here," he said. "I'll just be a moment."

BJ stared at the coroner's van, his mouth slightly open. "I don't understand," he whispered. He turned back to Maris, his eyes misty. "What happened?"

She slowly shook her head. "I'm afraid we don't know." Although Mac had mentioned poison, she decided to let him break that news, if indeed he would be sharing it.

"More than likely we'll have to wait for an autopsy."

"So he never got up?" BJ asked.

"No, he didn't," Maris said. "When I realized how late it had gotten, I went to check on him."

It was only when she'd spoken those words that a thought occurred to her. If she'd checked earlier, would Reggie still be alive? She pushed the thought from her mind. Before she started second guessing herself, she'd wait to see what the coroner said about the time of death.

BJ seemed to be recovering a bit of his color but his lips looked like they were sticking to his teeth.

"I'm going to get a glass of water," she said, not bothering to ask if he wanted one. When she returned, she brought two.

"Thanks," he said as he took it from her. "I came back early because I thought maybe we could go do something together." He took a long drink of water, and was setting down his glass when Mac returned.

"BJ," he said, opening his notepad. "Could you give me your full name?"

"Barney Jaeger Ridder," he said. "It's Danish. But everyone's called me BJ since I was born."

"And how long have you known Reggie?" the sheriff asked.

"Since freshman year in college," BJ said. "We were gaming buddies. Actually, we still game...or gamed."

"What is it that you do at..." He checked his notes. "Whiz Kid Games?"

"I'm a game developer," he said. When Mac raised his brows, he added, "I invent the games, write them, come up with the rules, create the world."

"How long have you been at the company?" Mac asked.

BJ shrugged. "Since the beginning really. It was my game that got us our first big hit."

"How many years?" Mac asked.

BJ thought for a moment. "Over twenty... I'd say twenty-three or twenty-four years."

"I understand there was some disagreement over a game last night," the sheriff said.

BJ grimaced. "Oh that. It wasn't over the game itself." He glanced at Maris and then back to Mac. "It was more that we all thought we were having a company off-site just to kind of relax. We'd been pushing super hard on the game."

"But Reggie wanted you to work?"

BJ shook his head. "Not exactly. It was a play test, sort of a last minute quality check. The game itself is done."

Mac finished jotting down a note and closed the pad. "After the play test ended, where were you last night?"

"Where was I?" he asked, blinking at the sheriff. His gaze flicked to the ceiling. "In my room. We all went to our rooms." Then his eyes widened and he stared at Mac. "Wait. Why does it matter where I was?"

"Reggie Atkinson died under suspicious circumstances." He paused for a moment, watching BJ. "I'll be questioning everyone who was in the house."

"But...but," BJ sputtered again. "I thought he died in his sleep."

Mac put away his notepad. "We won't know until the autopsy report is back."

At that moment, the coroner appeared in the door, and Mac turned to him. They moved into the hallway out of earshot.

"Do the others know yet?" BJ asked.

"No," Maris said. "It's probably best to tell

them when they return. It's going to come as a bit of a shock." While that was true, seeing their reactions might be important too.

BJ nodded. "Right, right," he said quietly.

Just then Maris heard the metal ratchet of the coroner's gurney. She stood. "Let's wait on the back porch," she told BJ. She'd seen in similar circumstances how the removal of the body could be a difficult moment to see.

"Okay, sure," he said.

They moved out onto the back porch just in time. As BJ shielded his eyes to look up at the lighthouse, the coroner's team moved the gurney—laden with its large black body bag —through the hallway. By the time BJ turned around, the body was gone and Mac was joining them out on the porch.

"Mr. Ridder?" he said.

"Yes?"

Maris heard the coroner's van start up.

"I'd like you to stay in town," the sheriff said, "in case I need to ask you more questions." He handed the game developer a business card. "If you remember anything else, anything that seems even remotely relevant, please don't hesitate to call me."

BJ stared down at the card. "Okay," he

said quietly. "We're staying the weekend any-way, I guess."

Mac turned to Maris. "Forensics is done, so the room is yours. I'm heading over to Plateau 7. When the other guests return, could you let me know?"

"I'll do that," she said, nodding, and watched him go.

BJ sank onto one of the deck chairs and stared out to sea, though Maris had the distinct impression he wasn't seeing it. Earlier, she had sat on the front porch with much the same expression. He might need a few moments alone.

"I'm going to see if Cookie can whip up one of her famous restorative teas," Maris said to him, and headed to the kitchen.

8
———

By the time Bear arrived to work on the new greenhouse, BJ had gone upstairs to lie down—helped by Cookie's tea. You could rest assured that when she brewed something for you, it was precisely what you needed, even if that was simply some rest.

Maris spent her time changing all the sheets and towels in Reggie's room. It helped to stay busy and she didn't want the others to have to see an unmade bed where he had died. The forensics team had taken his possessions and luggage. She presumed that Mac would find a way to contact the next of kin.

When she was done, she threw open the window to the warm afternoon breeze before going downstairs. Cookie had decided to cope with the stress of their guest's death in her own way: making a late lunch for them all. She gathered everyone on the back porch where the table was already set.

"Cookie," Maris said taking a seat. "What in the world have you wrought?"

"Fillet of cod sandwiches," the chef said. "Dig in."

As usual, Bear Orsino had two sandwiches entirely for himself, and wasted not a moment tucking a napkin into the front of his t-shirt. Their mountain of a handyman had an appetite that matched his outsized form. Though his blue bib overalls stretched a bit over his burgeoning middle, it was his strong legs and big arms that gave him his larger than life look. He wore his thick brown hair closely cropped but his beard was thick and full.

"Thank you, Cookie," the big man said. He picked up a sandwich and took a big bite. His eyes widened as he chewed and nodded.

Though she wasn't particularly hungry, Maris picked up her sandwich and at least enjoyed its presentation. Two halves of a French baguette where filled with a grilled white fillet of cod, accompanied by thin wedges of avocado, a slice of heirloom tomato, and a leaf of butterhead lettuce. Though the morning's stress had unsettled her stomach, she also didn't want to disappoint Cookie.

As Maris bit into the crunch of the baguette and lettuce, the first sensation was its perfect temperature. Both the bread and cod fillet were warm, contrasting with the cool of the tomato. The tender fish melted in her mouth, and the avocado lent a contrasting smooth texture that was lovely. When she could speak again, she said to Cookie, "Salt, pepper, and a little something extra."

Cookie winked at her, setting her own sandwich down. "A little paprika."

"Ah," Maris said nodding. "Yes, that's it."

Cookie gazed at the patch of ground just beyond the large herb garden. "You're making an amazing amount of progress over there."

From her vantage point, Maris could see that Bear had used hexagonal cement paving stones in crimson, gray, and a light buff to lay a pretty, patterned floor for the small building.

He nodded as he swallowed, then wiped his mouth and beard with the napkin. "The floor is done."

"Done?" Cookie said, grinning.

Bear nodded. "The frame comes next. Then the glass. Everything is in the truck."

Cookie exchanged a surprised look with Maris, before turning back to Bear.

"You, my friend," the chef said, "are amazing."

Pink rose in his cheeks and he ducked his head a little, but he said nothing as he got back to work on his lunch.

Despite her stomach—or maybe because of it—Maris had already gone through half of her sandwich as well. Not only had lunch been late and the sandwich delicious but she had always been a stress eater. Unfortunately, it'd taken her years to figure it out. Though she'd been good about avoiding chocolate since returning to Pixie Point Bay, it hadn't been that hard. The diminutive chef rarely cooked with it, and Maris had managed to stop buying it. But it was times like these that made her wish she still had a secret stash. She ought to save half her sandwich for later, but she already knew she wouldn't.

"I can speak with Pammy and Felix when they return," Cookie said to her.

Without realizing it, Maris had stopped eating and had been looking out at the ocean. "No that's all right," she said, giving Cookie a little smile. "But thank you. I think it might come better from me, because...well, you know."

Though Bear was still munching through his first baguette, his big brown eyes flicked back and forth between her and Cookie. Maris realized he didn't know about Reggie.

"One of our guests died last night," she said. Bear stopped eating in mid-chew, and his bushy eyebrows arched high. "Reggie Atkinson. He booked the B&B for himself and his three employees, one of whom is resting upstairs, but the other two have yet to return."

Bear set his sandwich down, as he gulped his last mouthful. "I'm sorry," he said, his shoulders hunching as he stared at the table.

"What did the sheriff say?" Cookie asked.

Maris sighed and sat back. "He suspects poison, which is why we had to gather everything up, but he won't know anything until the remains in the wine glass are analyzed and the autopsy results come back."

"I assume that the employees are suspects?" the chef asked. "They seemed pretty unhappy last night."

"Honestly," Maris said, "I imagine we all are, including Chef Fournier. But since none of us would have had a motive, Mac won't waste time with us, beyond a few questions to fill in the facts."

Cookie snorted and nodded to the bay, in the direction of Plateau 7. "Be prepared for fireworks from a certain French chef when he's questioned." She looked at the sandwiches that Bear and Maris hadn't finished. "Come on you two." She indicated their plates. "Keep up your strength."

Though Maris and Bear both picked up their baguettes, they both ate with less gusto.

"Have I told you about the first plantings that I have planned for our new Victorian greenhouse?" Cookie asked no one in particular. "Basil seedlings. I've always wanted to grow my own seedlings."

As Cookie chatted about the different plants, the care they needed, and how she would use them, Bear listened intently and ate his second sandwich, while Maris completely finished her first. The B&B's chef had obviously changed the topic of conversation to lighten the mood, but Maris didn't care. It had worked. She found herself picturing the new plants, and how cute the seedlings would be in tiny pots. As the meal concluded, Cookie pointed to the paving stones.

"Show me what you've done, young man," she said to Bear.

Nimble for such a big man, Bear quickly got out of his seat and helped Cookie out of hers.

As Maris collected the plates, she said, "Thank you, Cookie—for everything."

The chef gave her a wink before following Bear to the herb garden.

In the late afternoon, as Maris was vacuuming the library, Pammy and Felix came in from the back porch. In their t-shirts, shorts, and sun hats, they were laughing and sporting new tans. It looked like the kayaks had been a hit. As Maris turned off the vacuum, the pair stopped.

"Thanks for recommending the kayaks," Pammy said. "We had a wonderful time."

"Exhausting," Felix said, "but really fun."

"We made it all the way past the pier–" she began.

"And then on to the tidal pools," he finished. "They were so cool. We saw these little..." He glanced at Pammy. "I don't know what you'd call them. Maybe little guppies or something?"

She lifted her shoulders. "Who knows, but they were super cute."

Felix laughed. "If you like swimming baby worms."

Though Maris hated to bring them down from their outing high, there wasn't going to be any good way to break the news.

"I'm glad I caught you both," she said, moving the vacuum aside. "Would you mind taking a seat for a minute?" For a moment the two of them just looked at her, as though she'd spoken a foreign language. When neither of them moved, she said, "I'm afraid I have some bad news."

"What?" Felix said, frowning. "Has Reggie decided to cancel the weekend?"

"Oh, geez," Pammy said, her brow furrowing as she let her arms flop down to her sides.

"No," Maris said, "nothing like that." She sat down in one of the high back chairs to encourage them. "Please." She indicated the couch across from her.

"Okay," Felix said cautiously, but he went to a chair.

"I feel like we broke some rule or something," Pammy muttered, but she sat down as well.

"I'm afraid I have some bad news about Reggie," Maris said, swallowing in a suddenly dry throat. "I found him earlier this afternoon." She looked at them both. "He died in his bed sometime last night or this morning."

Felix sat bolt upright. "What?"

Pammy shook her head as though to clear it. "Wait. What?"

Footsteps in the hallway made them all look to the doorway, where BJ appeared. His grim and beleaguered expression said it all.

"Oh no," Pammy whispered, and covered her mouth with both hands.

"What happened?" Felix said, gaping at BJ, who only shrugged his shoulders and then took the nearest seat, on an ottoman.

"The authorities are investigating," Maris told him. "There's going to be some forensics results, as well as an autopsy."

"Oh my god," Pammy gasped.

"Why?" Felix demanded.

"He died under 'suspicious circumstances'," BJ said, using air quotes. "The sheriff asked me not to leave town."

"Oh wow," Felix said, sitting back. Eyes

wide, he looked at each one of them in turn. "I can't believe this."

Pammy's eyes teared up. "Are you sure?" she said to Maris. "I mean… Oh god." Quietly, she began to cry.

Maris quickly fetched a tissue from a nearby box. "I'm afraid I'm quite sure, Pammy." She handed her the tissue and set the box on the coffee table. "I'm sorry for your loss." She gazed around the room. "All of you."

For a few minutes the only sound was Pammy weeping and an occasional sniff.

"Could it have been a heart attack or a stroke?" Felix finally said.

"How could you tell just by looking?" BJ asked.

Felix shrugged. "I don't know. He was pretty overweight."

"He was still a young man," Pammy protested. She took off her glasses and wiped her eyes.

"Since I'm the same age," BJ said, "I agree." He shook his head and looked at the floor. "We knew each other for a long time. Over twenty-five years."

"Wow," Felix said. "I didn't know you guys went that far back."

Just then a tiny, tinny harmonica-like meow drew Maris's attention to the hallway. Mojo stood there, his big orange eyes fixed on hers. Then he turned and trotted off down the hall.

As the three colleagues continued their conversation, moving on to discuss the previous evening, Maris slipped from the room.

10

———

Out in the hallway, Maris was just in time to see Mojo disappear into the living room. As she followed him, she had to frown a little. She'd felt sure he was beckoning her to the parlor, where he could have jumped on the Ouija board to spell out a clue or used the tarot deck. If ever she needed a clue about a murder, it was now. But instead the little black cat jumped up on an embroidered chair, then its back, and finally up to the mantle of the fireplace. He took up a seat between the matching potpourri vases, his eyes nearly level with hers.

"Mojo," she admonished him. "I thought you were going to help."

As if in answer, he went to one of the ornate vases and pawed it.

"*No*," Maris exclaimed, as it tipped from the shelf. She dashed forward and lunged, stretching out her arms and fingers. As potpourri flew through the air and pelted her face, she made a desperate grab for the vase. As she sat down hard on the floor, the porcelain landed in her palm, then bobbled for a second until her other hand clamped down on it. As though she were playing football, she hugged it to her stomach.

"Good grief," she gasped.

Both of the vases were antiques. She held it out from her and looked all over it. It seemed completely undamaged.

"Mojo," she muttered, "if this had–" Something amidst the scattered dried flowers and herbs caught her eye. "What?" It was a tarot card. Her brows furrowed as she reached over to pick it up. It must have been inside the vase. She turned it around.

"The Knight of Cups," she murmured.

Against a background of orange mountains and a winding blue stream, an armored and helmeted knight rode on a beautiful white horse. In his hand he carried a golden goblet. Maris checked the doorway to the living room before she discreetly tapped her temple. Using her photographic memory she brought up the tarot interpretation booklet.

According to the description, the knight wore a brightly colored cloak covered with images of fish, the symbol of water, consciousness, and creativity. Both his helmet and boots were winged, in order to symbolize active and creative imagination as well as an appreciation for beautiful things.

"Hmm," she said, as she looked more closely at the card. Finally she spotted the small fish and the wings on the boots. She pursed her lips remembering how the card had fallen. It'd been inverted. Calling up the booklet again she read that, in the reversed position, the Knight of Cups meant that a creative project was emerging but that its creator was not yet ready to act on it.

"A creative project," she said. Was it referring to the murder-mystery game that they'd played last night? As she scooped the potpourri back into the vase, she thought about the golden cup. Could it represent poison?

She gazed up to the mantle where Mojo was watching her intently. With a little wave of the card, she said, "Sorry I doubted you." How he'd gotten the card into the vase, she couldn't quite imagine, but he'd done it.

Once she was sure she'd gathered all the potpourri, she got up and put the vase back in its place. Then she gently took Mojo from the mantle where he sat—as though he was waiting for her.

She put her lips against the soft fur between his ears. "Next time, try not to destroy the antiques," she whispered. His only reply was to purr. "Come on," she said to him, heading out. "Let's go text Mac that the others have returned. Then we can put away this card."

11

Late afternoon at the B&B meant a warm breeze from the sea, and the usual healthy dose of sunshine. Maris had decided to take advantage of the weather and wait for Mac outdoors. But rather than be in the sun, she took shelter on the B&B's front porch, rocking gently in the bench swing. Although a favorite with visiting children, and even a romantic couple or two, Maris had rarely taken the time to simply sit and rock. Though the view from the front of the house couldn't match the view from the back, Maris found herself enjoying it nonetheless.

The verdant hills just to the east hid the winding road to town. Beyond them, the coastal mountain range that was home to the redwoods rose up in dark tones of green. The two together reminded Maris of a resort in Switzerland where she'd once worked. At the time it had seemed like the set of a movie and yet now, it was the view from her porch.

The sheriff's SUV pulled off the coast highway in the distance, and eventually made it's way up the B&B's long gravel drive. Maris watched as Mac got out and greeted her with his usual smile.

"A welcoming committee," he said as he came up the steps. "I could get used to this."

She stood, smiling back. "You might have heard, but we're known for our hospitality here."

He tilted his head to her. "Within your dear mansion may wayward contention or withering envy ne'er enter."

Now she had to grin. "Robert Burns?" The sheriff had a fondness for the Scottish poet and frequently demonstrated his knowledge of the man's works.

Mac nodded. "I imagine that good old Rabbie would have appreciated your mansion." He glanced up at the gables, but as he looked at the front door his smile faded. "Are they all still here?"

"In the library," she said, nodding. "They all know that Reggie's dead. I told Pammy and Felix that he died under suspicious circumstances, but nothing more. I also didn't tell them that you were coming."

"Good," Mac said, regarding her. As they went to the entrance, he added, "We're going to make a deputy out of you yet." He opened the door for her and they went directly to the library. Though the threesome were talking quietly, the conversation died abruptly when she and Mac appeared in the doorway.

"Good afternoon," the sheriff said.

Although Felix and Pammy gaped at him, BJ said, "Good afternoon, sheriff."

Maris indicated Felix. "This is Felix Ong, and this is Pammy Sheehan. Along with BJ Ridder, they work at Whiz Kid Games and are staying with us."

Mac nodded to them. "Ms. Sheehan, may I speak to you alone?"

Her hand flew to her chest. "Me?" Her circular black glasses made her wide eyes seem even larger.

"I just have a few routine questions for you," he assured her.

BJ caught Felix's eye. "We'll be outside," he said, and nodded toward the porch door.

As the two men left, Pammy's gaze followed them with something that looked to Maris like longing combined with envy.

"Ms. Sheehan," Mac said, sitting opposite her and taking his notepad from his breast pocket. "How long had you known Reggie Atkinson?"

She brought her attention back to the sheriff. "Well, since I started at the company. I guess about seven years now."

"And what do you do there?" he asked, as Maris took a seat.

"I'm the artistic director," she said, but then shrugged. "Which anymore means the artist."

Mac gave her a quizzical look. "Anymore?"

"Back when I hired on, there was a small staff of artists, maybe three or four depending on the project. That was when the company was doing well. Now...it's just me."

"So the company isn't doing well?" he asked.

"Not like before, for sure." She tilted her head toward the porch. "BJ's hit game was what made the company. When sales eventually started to fade, we didn't have another hit."

"Not one?" Maris asked.

Pammy grimaced. "Not one."

Maris glanced outside, where the two men were sitting. "But you've still got all the same people who created the first one?"

The artist shrugged again. "Sure. But it's about the market too. What's hot right now. It's like trying to get lightning to strike twice." When Maris and Mac just looked at her, she added, "If game companies could predict what would be the next big hit, we'd all be doing it. But we don't—or at least *we* haven't."

"I'm surprised," Maris said. "When Reggie called, he was very clear that he wanted to reserve the entire B&B for the weekend. And a five course meal from Plateau 7 wouldn't be cheap either." She looked at Mac and then back to Pammy. "But you're saying the company isn't doing well."

Pammy shook her head. "I was surprised too. I mean..." She lowered her voice. "I haven't been paid my salary for two weeks."

As Mac made a note his eyebrows arched. "I thought maybe Reggie was going to announce some big sale coming down the pike."

Maris thought back to the dinner. "Didn't he though? He said he'd sold the game to... something or someone called Hario."

Pammy made a sour face. "Reggie punted. Hario is a competitor. He obviously didn't think we could get our distributors to order enough copies. Or maybe he didn't think it'd take off in the gaming community."

"So, this sale to Hario, would you call it a last ditch effort to save the company?" Mac asked.

The artist blew out some air, then lifted her hands. "Honestly, I don't really know what to call it. It's not really my area. I'm just an artist." But she paused as she thought of something and then dropped her hands. "An artist who is now out of a job."

"Where were you last night, after the game broke up?" the sheriff asked.

She blinked at him, her mouth falling open a bit. "Where was I?" She glanced at Maris. "Well, in my room, of course."

Mac nodded. "Were you alone?"

Her face flushed a vivid red. "Of course I was."

"How would you characterize your relationship with Mr. Atkinson?" the sheriff asked.

"We weren't in a relationship," she said vehemently.

Maris frowned a little. To quote a different poet, it seemed that Pammy "doth protest too much."

"I meant your work relationship," Mac said calmly.

"Oh." She blinked at him, then paused and took a breath. "Oh, right." She pursed her lips. "It was good."

"Never an argument about the art?" he asked. "No disagreements about anything?"

Pammy smiled sadly as she shook her head. "It's the best job I've ever had." Her voice began to tremble. "Reggie was...a great boss." She began to cry again, and Maris scooted the box of tissues closer to her. She quickly took one and put it to her nose.

"All right, Ms. Sheehan," Mac said standing. He gave Maris a look and nodded to the porch. "Thank you for your time." He took out a business card and put it on the table. "If there's anything else you remember that you think might be at all relevant, please contact me."

Maris stood as Pammy only nodded, and she and Mac headed to the back porch.

12

―――――――

"Looks like it's your turn," BJ said to Felix. "I'll be inside."

They'd been standing at the railing looking out at the bay. A few sailboats skimmed the sparkling blue waters, while someone on a jet ski nearer to shore kicked up a rooster tail of streaming water. A warm scented breeze wafted through Cookie's herb garden, while Bear worked on erecting the metal supports of the future greenhouse.

Maris eyed the structure. If he kept up this pace, he'd have it done by sunset. Then again, their shifter handyman liked to be home before dark. With the sun already sinking toward the west, he would likely be leaving soon.

As BJ went back inside, Mac said to Felix, "Mr. Ong, would you like to have a seat?"

"Honestly," Felix said, "I was sitting almost all day in a kayak. I'd prefer to stand."

Mac nodded. "Can you tell me where you were last night, after the game broke up?"

"Sure," he said. "I went to my room, and took my glass of Merlot with me. I finished it up there, while I looked at my phone. I was probably asleep within an hour." He looked at Mac and then Maris, frowning. "Why? Am I a suspect?"

"These are just routine questions, Mr. Ong," the sheriff said smoothly. "I'm asking everyone who was here to tell me about their whereabouts." He made a note. "I understand there was some heated discussion during dinner and also before the game ended."

Felix scowled. "You could say that." He crossed his arms over his chest. "We were all told it was going to be a company off-site— just for recreation. We'd been pushing hard on that game, and Reggie said we all needed a break. Then he pulled it out for a play test." He glanced at Maris then back to Mac. "I think we all felt a little betrayed."

"And angry?" Mac suggested.

"And angry," Felix said. "There's no point in denying it."

"How long have you been at Whiz Kid Games and what do you do there, Mr. Ong?"

"I joined a couple of years ago. I'm a producer," he shrugged his shoulders and dropped his hands. "The only producer at this point."

"And what does a producer do?" Mac asked.

"Production," Felix said curtly. But when Mac fixed him with a stern look, he quickly added, "Budget and schedule mostly. I handle all the contracts too. In my copious free time I also fact-check the games."

"Fact-checking would involve research?" Mac asked, still looking directly at him.

"Sure," Felix said. "Sometimes the worlds for the games are pretty obscure." He gestured to the B&B. "Like a Victorian period home: what it looks like, what they ate, what they wore. I have to fact-check everything."

"Then you must have researched the murder method in the game," Mac concluded. "Which, if I'm not mistaken, was poison. In fact, you likely know about many poisons for these types of games."

Felix crossed his arms again. "That was the first murder mystery game we've ever produced. All I know about poisons or the Victorian era is from that game—which isn't much."

As Mac made a note, Maris said, "Pammy told us that she hasn't been paid in a couple of weeks."

Felix grimaced. "Right. Me either." But when Mac finished with his notepad, he said, "And that's why none of us can be a suspect."

Mac tucked the pad in his breast pocket. "How do you figure?"

Felix nodded toward the library. "All of us had a vested interest in Reggie being alive. That game was his baby. He was the one pushing it. Besides, without him, there isn't really a company. Sure it wasn't doing well, but there was at least some light at the end of the tunnel." He shook his head. "Now, I'll be scrambling for a job."

"The light at the end of the tunnel," the sheriff said. "You're referring to the sale of the game to Hario?"

"Right," Felix said.

"Why would Pammy call that a punt?" Maris asked.

"Because he didn't trust his own team with it," Felix said. "He didn't think we could get distributors excited enough about it. Our last handful of games have been duds. So he sold it to a competitor, who probably got a deal on it. In return, Reggie got a quick cash influx to help the bottom line—and pay us."

As Mac handed him a business card, Maris took a mental note. Both Felix and Pammy had begun to worry about their jobs, no longer in shock over Reggie's death.

"If you can think of anything else that might be relevant to Mr. Atkinson's death," the sheriff said, "please let me know."

The producer took it and read it, before looking up at him. "I suppose we're all supposed to stay in town?"

Mac nodded. "I'd appreciate that, at least for the remainder of your reservation. Thanks for your time."

"Sure," Felix replied, before he headed inside.

Cookie passed him in the vestibule, as she headed out. She glanced at Maris.

"Thought I'd check with Bear before he leaves for the day."

"Cookie," the sheriff said, "good." He nodded to the greenhouse. "Would you join Maris and I?"

13

As Maris, Mac, and Cookie made their way to the back edge of the herb garden, Bear was packing up his tools and another gorgeous sunset was beginning over the ocean. Gossamer wisps of clouds blossomed from the horizon in a giant pink fan. It spread high over their heads and was reflected in the darkening bay below it.

Mac came to a stop just beyond the garden and not quite to the greenhouse. "Three disgruntled employees doesn't make a motive for murder."

Maris nodded and said to Cookie, "Apparently Pammy and Felix haven't been paid for two weeks."

Cookie scowled. "Haven't been paid? But Reggie rented the entire B&B." She glanced across the bay. "And had Chef Fournier cater a five-course meal."

"He said at dinner that he'd sold the murder mystery game to Hario," Maris noted. "So the money might have come from there."

"Except Pammy called that a punt," the sheriff said. When he saw Cookie's quizzical look, he added, "He sold the game to a competitor rather than publish it himself."

At the greenhouse, Bear unloaded several glass panels from a wheelbarrow and stacked them against the now complete metal structure. He put a large bag of tools in the empty barrow and headed back to his truck in the front.

"They were angry at dinner," the chef said, "but not that angry."

Maris shook her head. "I didn't think so either."

Mac looked at them both. "That was my sense of it as well. Being stiffed a couple weeks salary, or coming to play a game instead of having a vacation are good reasons to be upset, but not lethal." He hooked his thumbs behind his utility belt. "We don't have any test results back yet, but I'll bet dollars to donuts that someone put something in

Reggie's wine that killed him." He looked at them both. "Did anyone in particular have opportunity?"

As Bear returned with another load of glass, Maris said, "It was a long evening, and a complicated game. Everyone had their own character sheet and Reggie seemed to have a script."

Though she could have tapped her temple and brought up the evening, scene by scene, it would have been obvious.

Bear neatly stacked the glass, put the last of his tools in the wheelbarrow, and waved to them. Cookie and Maris waved back. "Thank you, Bear," Cookie called out to him.

"You're welcome," he said, and headed down the side of the house.

"Do you still have all the game materials?" Mac asked.

Maris shook her head. "Forensics does. They're with Reggie's belongings. He took them up to his room at the end of the evening."

Cookie snapped her fingers. "I know. We could re-enact it. Just run through it real quick."

Maris smiled at Cookie, who grinned

back at her. That was the perfect solution. She didn't have to use her photographic memory after all—at least not here and now.

Mac regarded the chef. "That's a good idea." He gazed at the sky, and the now blazing sunset. Against the deeply blue background of evening, the vibrant pink tendrils looked as though they were lit from within. "It's getting late though."

"And it's time for me to see to the Wine Down," Maris said.

Mac frowned a little. "The Wine Down?"

"The evening wine and cheese," she told him. "Affectionately known in the hospitality industry as the Wine Down."

He smiled and nodded. "Ah, gotcha."

"You're welcome to stay for it," she suggested.

Though he paused and seemed to be considering it, he finally shook his head. "I think that the county sheriff might put a damper on your guests." He glanced at the B&B. "Seeing as how they're all suspects."

Maris had to laugh a little. "Then I guess you'll just need to have your wine and cheese out here, and eavesdrop."

"Out here?" Mac replied, smiling. "Well,

as the poet once said, 'Any place is good for eavesdropping, if you know how to eavesdrop.'"

Maris's brows furrowed. "That doesn't sound like Burns."

Mac grinned at her. "Tom Waits." At her look of puzzlement he added, "Blues and folk singer extraordinaire."

She'd forgotten that the sheriff and her Aunt Glenda had both enjoyed the blues. "Maybe another time then."

He tilted his head toward her. "Another time." Then he checked his watch. "So tomorrow morning for the re-enactment?"

She nodded. "That sounds good."

Cookie said, "Breakfast finishes at ten."

"Right," the sheriff said, "I'll see you both then."

14

———

In the living room, BJ, Pam, and Felix were chatting. As Maris quietly entered, she turned on one of the Tiffany lamps and then went to the fireplace. She'd already laid the kindling and stacked the logs earlier in the day. Though the evening had yet to become cold or foggy, a light mist was drifting in from the bay, bringing with it a little chill. She struck one of the long matches on the holder's iron base and lit the fire.

"Oh how nice," Pammy said, watching Maris light the kindling. "I love a fire."

Maris stood and smiled at her. "Me too," she said. Then she took in the three of them. "Wine and cheese, perhaps in here tonight?"

It'd occurred to her that, given what had

happened the previous night, that the trio might not be interested in the Wine Down at all.

"That'd be great," Felix said.

BJ nodded. "I know I could use a glass."

Both Felix and Pammy muttered their agreement.

Maris nodded, glad that they were sticking together through this, and also glad that they were recovering from the shock. She tossed the long match stick into the fire. "Coming right up."

In the kitchen, Maris took out the oversize wooden cheese board, scored and stained from years of good service. Then she surveyed the cheeses in the fridge, keeping in mind the dry goods in the pantry as well as the wines in the cabinet and the cooler. Without overthinking it, a plan came together.

In her opinion a cheeseboard ought to have, at the most, four different cheeses. But four was plenty to showcase the local varieties from Cheeseman Village as well as provide a flavor and texture for every palette. She selected the triple cream Brie, the extra sharp six-year aged cheddar, a buttery

Gouda, and the nutty Manchego. She took these to the large butcher block before returning. As a compliment she also chose the green olives, a black olive tapenade, and a spicy brown mustard.

As she sliced the cheeses, her mind turned to the sweet part of the board. She arranged the cheeses and fetched Cookie's french baguette from the bread box, slicing thin slivers from it at a diagonal. From the pantry she brought a sweet chutney, the peach jam, and also candied pecans and dried apricots. With everything on the board, she stood back from it for a moment, hands on hips. Then she nodded to herself. Despite the grinding years in the hospitality industry, she never tired of the Wine Down. It was the last opportunity in the day to extend warmth and relaxation to guests.

When she took the cheeseboard into the living room and set it on the coffee table, there were appreciative murmurs all around.

"Oh my god," Pammy said. "This could be dinner."

Though Maris didn't say anything as she went to get the wine and glasses, she smiled to herself. In effect, that was the point. Sometimes the last thing that guests wanted to do was venture out yet again after coming in from a long day—particularly the guests of the B&B. Although the restaurants in town and in Cheeseman Village or even the wineries down south were all top notch—Maris enjoyed recommending them—they were a bit of a drive. Many of the tourists who visited the lighthouse were active people who liked the sightseeing and exercise that the environs provided. They'd often spend all the daylight hours seeing and doing as much as they could, not unlike the guests here tonight.

She took a Cabernet from the wine cabinet that would stand up to the aged cheddar, and from the pantry's wine cooler she chose a bright and fruity Sauvignon Blanc that would pair well with sweets. By the time she returned, Pammy was munching some of the Manchego dipped in spicy mustard. She'd moved to stand next to the fire, with her back to it. Maris showed them all the bottle labels. "Can I pour red or white for you?" she asked.

Red for Felix and BJ, and white for Pammy. She went to get the appropriate glasses from the dining room's sideboard, and took them into the living room. Though she'd occasionally run across wine enthusiasts who dismissed the use of different shaped glasses for the different wines, Maris found that it indeed made a difference. The wider and larger glasses for the reds allowed for more aeration and distance from the nose. The slightly narrower white wine glasses concentrated their delicate aroma and kept them cooler for longer.

It also helped the guests keep track of their glasses.

Outside, the sun had nearly sunk below the horizon and the white mist of the early fog took on a rosy glow. Maris knew that the lighthouse beam would be rotating now, and sometimes urged guests outside to take a look. But as she poured and distributed the wine, the little group was settling in with their food, and their conversation had resumed.

"You saw that new board game from Butler & Company?" Felix said before sipping his wine.

BJ was coating a piece of bread with the chutney, but paused and looked at Felix. "They have a new board game? Since when?"

"Since two days ago," Felix said. "It's tearing up the charts."

"The one about the Maya ruins and digging up treasure?" Pammy asked.

"That's the one," Felix said, pointing at her. Then he rolled his eyes. "I can hardly imagine the amount of research on that one."

"The artwork is to die for," she said. "What a fun project that must have been."

Maris poured herself a Sauvignon Blanc. "Did you say charts?" she asked Felix.

The producer had just popped a slice of cheese in his mouth but nodded.

"There are web sites that sell all kinds of games," BJ said. "They all have bestseller charts, and also the highest rated. They're not always the same."

Felix crooked his thumb at BJ. "This guy had his game in the top ten for months. *Months*. Should have won Game of the Year."

Maris raised her eyebrows as she went to stand with Pammy. "It sounds like a hit," she said smiling. "What was it about?"

BJ shrugged. "Classic RPG but a mafia setting." When he saw Maris's puzzled look, he added, "RPG, role playing game. Everyone takes on a character, but the game play is around a table."

"You roll dice," Pammy said. "Sometimes there's a map or tokens." Although Maris nodded, she couldn't quite picture it. "It was definitely a hit but...that was a while ago."

"Yeah," BJ sighed.

There was silence in the room as the little group seemed to be remembering better days. But then Felix finished what remained in his wine glass and got up to refill it. Maris could already see that there wasn't a full glass left in the bottle.

"Would everyone like another Cabernet?" she asked. "Or would you enjoy something else?"

Felix poured what was left in the bottle. "This was great. It gets my vote." He looked at BJ. "Another one?"

BJ toasted him. "Sounds good."

By the time Maris returned with the opened bottle, Felix had already finished his glass. She poured him another, a full one this time. As she offered to pour for BJ, he declined but Felix took a big, loud gulp.

"Geez, Felix," Pammy said. "You're going to drink poor Maris here out of business."

Although Maris was about to tell them about buying in bulk from the wineries down south, Felix picked up the small cheese knife from the board and clinked it against the side of his glass a few times.

"Attention everybody," he said, a touch dramatically. "Can I have your attention, please? I have an announcement I'd like to make."

15

Maris took a step back, in front of the fireplace, as Felix took center stage in the living room. Pammy and BJ exchanged puzzled and bemused looks. But Felix stood up a bit straighter, looked at Pammy and BJ, and then cleared his throat.

"This is something that I've been working on for a long time," he said, but paused and looked down into his wine glass. He stroked his goatee once. "I just didn't know when to say something, but I guess there's no sense in waiting now." He took a deep breath and looked up at them. "I'm starting my own company."

"What?" Pammy said, just as BJ said, "You're what?"

Felix held a hand up to them. "I know, I know. But that's not all." They both fell silent. "I want you guys to be my partners."

"But–" BJ began.

"I've already got the money," Felix said, stopping him. "I'm fully capitalized for the first year."

"Money?" Pammy asked. "For a year? How did you do that?"

Felix nodded, as though he'd been hoping someone would ask. "That's what's taken me so long. I wrote the most detailed business plan that the Small Business Administration has ever seen. It took me months of research and writing, working on calendars and ideas, and spreadsheets and projections. It's been like an entire second job." He glanced at each of them. "But I got the word last week. I've been awarded an SBA loan."

"Wow," Pammy said. "Those are super hard to get."

Felix grinned at her. "Like extremely hard."

"What's the name of the company?" she asked.

"I'm tentatively calling it Power Play," he

said, "but that was just for the SBA. It'll be up to all of us. I'm not interested in dictating how we do things. You guys will have complete creative control. I'll bring the business side, all the usual production stuff, and we'll share in the profits equally." He quickly held up his hand again. "But don't give me your answer now. I want you guys to think about this. When we get back home, I can show you the business plan."

Pammy shook her head. "I don't want to see a business plan." She beamed at him. "I'm in."

Felix blinked at her and cocked his head back. "Awesome!"

Naturally, all eyes fell on BJ.

But Maris had been watching the game developer, ever since Felix had cut him off. The jaw muscles at the side of his face were working overtime, and his lips had pressed into a thin line. Now he turned a glare on Felix that should have melted the producer's wine glass.

"How can you be so...so callous?" BJ ground out through clenched teeth. "The man hasn't been dead twenty-four hours."

It was as though the temperature in the

room had ratcheted up several degrees. Quietly Maris stepped away from the fire, watching the trio.

"It doesn't have anything to do with Reggie," Felix protested, though he sounded less sure of himself.

"Really?" BJ barked at him. "Really? If he were alive, would we even be having this conversation? Were you going to invite *him* to be a part of your company?"

Felix's face fell. "Well, no," he admitted. "I wasn't thinking of it."

"He wasn't just our boss," BJ said, still seething. "He was our friend." He put his glass on the coffee table. "At least he was mine."

Felix opened his mouth as though he might protest, but then shut it.

BJ stood and looked at Maris. "Thank you for the wine and cheese."

Then without glancing at Felix or Pammy, he stalked out of the room. They heard him stomp up the stairs and then his bedroom door slammed shut.

For several moments the only sound was the crackling of the fire, but then Pammy said lowly, "Don't worry about BJ.

He's hurting right now. He'll come around."

Felix hung his head. "He's right, though. That was callous. I don't know what I was thinking." He regarded his wine glass, and purposefully set it aside, frowning. He glanced at Pammy and Maris, his face a bright red. "Sorry I ruined the evening," he said weakly, before hurrying from the room.

Pammy sighed heavily. "Well," she said to Maris, as she put her glass down too. "I'm still in, because where else am I going to go?"

Then she left as well.

Maris sighed and looked down at the barely touched spread. As she picked it up, Mojo appeared in the doorway and trotted over to rub his sides against her leg. She smiled down at him.

"Were you waiting for them to leave?" she asked him. Though he didn't answer in words, the fluffy black cat purred as he circled around her ankles. She chuckled a little. "Must be time to call it a night."

She took the glasses to the kitchen and loaded them in the dishwasher, Mojo staying close. Though he hadn't gone to sit by his bowl, Maris decided it was time for a treat.

She opened the fridge and took a little pinch of smoked salmon from the container. Mojo eagerly took it from her fingers.

As he snacked, she fetched the cheeseboard. While she put away the leftovers and washed the board, he used his paw to wash his face. But as Maris set the board aside to dry, she thought about Felix's timing.

With the award of the SBA loan, just before arriving at the B&B, Reggie had in effect become the producer's competitor. Given BJ's long history with his friend, had Felix really thought that the game developer would leave Whiz Kid Games? She wondered if, like Pammy and Felix, he hadn't been paid his salary either.

She pursed her lips, turned off the light in the kitchen, and bent to pick up Mojo—who immediately began to purr. As she headed to her room, carrying her warm little bundle, she put her lips to the soft fur at the top of his head.

"It's not making sense," she murmured, "at least not yet."

16

"Well," Maris said to Cookie, "at least they're eating."

It was one of the more awkward breakfasts she could remember. As though the three game designers were on some sort of rotation schedule, each had come down separately, loaded their plates, and then gone to a separate porch: Pammy to the front porch, Felix to the back, and BJ to the porch on the south side of the building, under the balcony.

Cookie was serving herself one of her signature scrambles: soft scrambled eggs combined with shredded Gruyere cheese, red potatoes, and thin sliced scallions. The morning buffet also had fresh cranberry

muffins, accompanied by just-picked straw-
berries, and they both were having tea. Maris
took a seat at the table with the chef, and recounted what had happened during the
Wine Down.

Cookie frowned a little. "That was poor
timing." She broke off part of the muffin's top.
"To say the least. Maybe even a touch in-
sensitive."

Maris tilted her head a little as she dug
into the scramble with her fork. "Honestly, I
think Felix was just excited. He was pretty
upset when he realized what he'd done." She
took a bite. The eggs, soft cheese, and scallions were luscious. "Mmm," she muttered,
nodding at Cookie. "Wonderful."

Just then, there was the sound of tires on
the gravel in front. Maris stood, poked her
head into the hallway, and saw through the
door's window that the sheriff's SUV was
parking in front. Back at the table, she
quickly dabbed her mouth with a napkin and
took a sip of tea. "It's Mac," she said to
Cookie.

"Oh right," the chef said, her black eyes
lighting up. "The re-enactment."

Maris met Mac just inside the front door's vestibule. "Good morning," she said, with her usual cheer.

"Good morning," he said, as he came in. He used his thumb to point back over his shoulder. "Isn't it a little foggy to be eating outside?"

Maris gestured for him to come inside. "There's been a bit of a falling out." She led the way to the dining room. "Breakfast is served. Please help yourself."

As Mac entered his smiled broadened. "That smells absolutely delicious. Good morning, Cookie."

"Good morning, Sheriff," she said and indicated the buffet. "Eggs scrambled with cheese, potatoes, and scallions."

Though he grinned at her, he shook his head. "Much as I'd like to, I'm afraid I've had my breakfast." He glanced at the carafe. "But is that coffee?"

"Yes indeed," the chef said.

As Mac poured his coffee, Maris returned to her breakfast. It hadn't escaped her notice that he had a manila folder tucked under his arm, and also a large envelope with a button and string clasp. Though he lingered next to the scramble, he moved past the warming trays and took a seat. He obviously hadn't remained fit and trim by overeating.

"Next time you pay a visit at breakfast time," Maris suggested, "plan on having something to eat here. I guarantee it'll be worth the wait."

Mac smiled at them both. "Well, thank you. I think I'll do that." He took a sip of his coffee and slid the manila folder forward. "I've got two things to share this morning. Neither as good as this coffee." He opened the folder. "A search warrant and the autopsy report. The county crime scene unit will be here later to conduct the searches."

"A search warrant?" Maris said. "I assume that's because of the autopsy results."

Mac nodded. "The autopsy report is on top." Maris quickly scanned it.

Cookie set down her tea. "Searches? What could you possibly be looking for?"

"Nitrobenzene," Maris and Mac said together. She'd placed her finger on the word near the bottom of the report.

"It was most definitely murder," the

sheriff said. "The blood work revealed nitrobenzene in Reggie's blood. I'd thought maybe cyanide because the residue in the wine glass smelled bitter. But the coroner tells me it would have tasted just like a sweet wine, except with almonds added."

"Almonds," Cookie said slowly, her gaze drifting toward the kitchen.

"So it was nitrobenzene in the wine glass too?" Maris asked.

Mac nodded. "Confirmed by the forensics team."

"Almonds," Cookie declared. "It was on the tip of my tongue. Tarte aux Amandes. It's what we had for dessert, a classic French almond tart."

Mac arched his eyebrows at her. "Interesting."

"The sweet smell of the dessert was everywhere that evening," Maris added.

"And it was quite good," Cookie said.

The sheriff smiled at her. "So we have the method now, nitrobenzene in the wine. And the opportunity, during the mystery game. But what we still lack is the motive."

"Well," Maris said, lowering her voice, "as

far as motive goes, something developed last night during the Wine Down. It's why Pammy is eating out in front, BJ under the balcony, and Felix out back."

"Oh?" Mac said, closing over the manila folder.

"It turns out that Felix is starting his own gaming company," Maris said. "He's asked both Pammy and BJ to be his partners. BJ was extremely upset with the timing of Felix's business move, although Felix said he'd been working for months to get an SBA loan—which was approved last week. But by accepting the loan and starting his own company, it seems to me that Whiz Kid Games was no longer Felix's employer, but his competition."

"Also interesting," the sheriff said. "Especially since the murder would have to have been premeditated. Someone had to have brought the poison with them, and then waited for an opportunity."

"I guess they found it," Cookie said. Since both she and Maris had finished their breakfasts, the chef stood, picked up her plate and Maris's as well. "Well, you two young whippersnappers," she said in her tremulous old woman voice. "Shall we?"

Though Mac seemed a bit surprised, he undid the tie string on the large envelope and took out the gaming booklets. "Ready when you are."

17

By the time Maris returned to the dining room, Pammy was coming back as well, bringing a mostly full plate. Maris noted the red rimming the artist's eyes behind her big round glasses. She stopped in the hallway and ducked her head when she saw Maris, then looked down at her plate.

"Sorry about the wasted food," she said quietly. "I guess I wasn't as hungry as I thought."

"No worries at all," Maris told her as she took the plate. "Cookie composts for her garden."

Pammy smiled a little. "Oh good." She noticed the game pamphlets on the dining room table. "The game," she said, her brows lifting. Then she frowned. "Are you going to play it?"

Mac must have heard them from the dining room, since he chose that moment to join them. "Not exactly," he said. "We're going to re-enact it."

Startled, Pammy put a hand to her chest. "Oh, I see."

Maris heard the back porch door, and a moment later Felix appeared in the living room's doorway, looking at them all. He held an empty plate, as well as his coffee cup. He paused, looking as if he'd interrupted something.

"Mr. Ong," Mac said. "I'd appreciate it if you'd join us. I have some information for everyone, as well as a request."

He could hardly meet Pammy's gaze, but she indicated the pamphlets in the dining room. "They want to do a re-enactment of the game," she said to him.

"Actually," Mac said, "the whole evening." As Cookie returned from the kitchen, she took the plates from Maris and Felix. "We're just missing Mr. Ridder," the sheriff said.

Maris nodded. "He's eating out on the side porch. I'll go see if he's done."

Outside, she found him looking at his phone, as usual. "BJ?" she said to him, prompting him to turn it off, "the sheriff is here with some new information. I wonder if you could join us inside?"

"Sure," he said, shrugging. "It's not like I have anything better to do." He stood and picked up his plate. "Autopsy results?" he asked, matter-of-factly.

Maris followed him inside. "Yes, that's right." It seemed that the game developer had calmed down since last night's angry tirade.

Inside, Mac had gathered everyone in the living room. "Mr. Ridder," he said. "Good." Then he removed the manilla folder from under his arm.

As Maris deposited BJ's empty plate in the kitchen, Cookie finished loading the dishwasher. As they completed the cleanup, Maris could hear Mac going over the same forensics and autopsy reports that they'd reviewed earlier. By the time she and Cookie joined them, the questions had started.

"What in the hell is nitrobenzene?" BJ asked.

"It's a solvent," Mac said, "mostly used in combination with other things."

"What other things?" Felix said.

"Household polishes and cleaners, for example," the sheriff told him.

"In his glass?" Pammy said, making an awful face. "How could he have drunk it?"

Mac tucked the manilla folder back under his arm. "It would have tasted sweet and smelled like almonds."

"You're kidding," Felix said, frowning. "Then none of us would have been able to taste it."

"Exactly," the sheriff said.

"But who would have known we'd be having an almond dessert?" BJ asked, glancing around at everybody. Mac turned to Cookie and Maris, his eyebrows arched.

Cookie shook her head. "We didn't know until the chef announced it."

"The only one who might possibly have known was Reggie," Maris said. "All we knew was that Plateau 7 would be catering."

Mac took out his notepad and jotted down something quick. "All right then." He closed it and looked at them all. "Felix and BJ, I've already mentioned to Pammy that we're going to re-enact the game that you all played that evening. It'll help me to get a better idea of everyone's whereabouts. It'll only take about an hour, if you three have the time."

BJ only shrugged, but Pammy said, "I haven't made any plans." Then she looked at the floor. "It didn't seem right."

"Me either," Felix said. "We were *all* supposed to be having fun."

"Was that before or after you decided to make your own company?" BJ said snidely.

"BJ," Pammy said, sounding exasperated. "Could you just drop it?"

In the tense silence that followed, Maris fetched the gaming pamphlets from the dining room and started passing them out.

"Did anyone leave the dining room during the meal?" Mac asked.

Everyone paused for a moment, then shook their heads.

"You couldn't have pulled me away with a tractor," Cookie said, making everyone murmur in agreement.

"It really was good," Pammy agreed.

"Say what you will," Felix put in, "Reggie knew food." There were nods of agreement from Pammy and BJ.

Maris added, "The only one who came

and went was Chef Fournier. He was staging the courses in the kitchen."

"How long did dinner last?" the sheriff asked.

Again there was silence, until BJ said, "Not long enough."

"I'd estimate," Cookie said, "about two-and-a-half hours, tops." She gazed around the room and got a few nods of agreement.

"All right," Mac said, looking at his pamphlet, "take me through this."

For the next hour, they all positioned themselves in the various rooms and went through their movements, made easier to remember by the game books. Maris served invisible wine in real glasses, and everyone tried to remember where they'd seen them during the evening, particularly Reggie's. As Mac occasionally took Reggie's position on the floor, even Mojo joined in again.

From time to time, they all spoke their character's lines and the sheriff would visit the different rooms, noting locations, people, and glasses, in order of game play. Maris noted that little real conversation took place today, unlike during the actual game. But despite the fact that it was just a quick run-through, it felt complete.

In the end, however, the sheriff had to conclude what Maris had already suspected. There'd been virtually no time in the evening when they'd all been together—until they'd quit. In fact, there'd been ample opportunity for each of them to have circulated unseen by most of the other players. Not even Maris and Cookie could swear to the other's location for the entire evening. As Reggie had intended, the game had used the Victorian B&B to its full.

"I'd say this was a bust," Felix said, tossing his pamphlet to the coffee table. "In terms of game play, it works well. It was designed to get people moving around and coming together in little groups. It's a shame we weren't going to publish it."

Mac got up from the floor, as Mojo gave a plaintive little meow. The sheriff gave him a scratch behind the ears. As he straightened, he picked up the glass and said, "Thanks for your time, everyone. I appreciate the help."

There was a knock at the front door. When Maris went to the hallway, she saw who it was. "Mac, the crime scene team is here."

As she went to let them in, she could hear Pammy behind her. "Crime scene team? What are they going to do?"

"I have a search warrant," the sheriff replied. "The team is going to search the premises."

18

As Maris and Mac looked on from the second floor's large hallway, the crime scene unit went methodically from one room to another. Cookie had returned to the kitchen, and Pammy, BJ, and Felix had decided to wait downstairs. Maris could hear quiet murmurs of their conversation. Though she couldn't make out any distinct words, their tone seemed to have returned to polite.

"There's really very little chance that they'll find anything at this point," Mac said, arms crossed as he watched through the doorway. "But we've got to give it a shot."

Maris thought back to how she'd washed everything in Reggie's room. It hadn't occurred to her that she might be destroying evidence. It'd just seemed the right thing to do so that the other guests didn't see the rumpled sheets and an unmade bed.

"When I made Reggie's bed..."

Mac held up a hand. "No worries there. The forensics team had been over everything. They gave me the all clear." He fixed his gray eyes on her, smiling. "And I gave the all clear to you."

They both returned to watching the search. In each of the guest rooms, the two female investigators methodically went through everything: from the luggage and dressers to the trash can. Though cameras and evidence bags stood by, nothing of suspicion or importance had yet turned up.

Even so, the gloved investigators in their dark blue windbreakers remained alert. The younger blonde went through the trash and looked under the bed, while the older, heavier brunette went through the contents of the luggage and also everything the bathroom. She opened every bottle and sniffed it, no matter if it was shampoo or mouthwash.

It seemed that none of the guests had used the dressers, although they'd all hung clothes in the armoires.

The team had already searched BJ and Felix's room, and seemed to be almost finished with Pammy's.

"Sheriff," said the younger woman from inside Pammy's room. "I think you should have a look at this."

He immediately strode inside and Maris shifted sideways for a better view. The young lady held up what looked like some sort of black cloth in her gloved hand. Mac peered at it as she turned it around so he could see it from different angles.

"Men's socks," she said.

"Yes," Mac said, glancing around the room. "Where did you find them?"

"In the bed," the other woman said, pointing to the bottom of it. "Under the sheets, at the very bottom."

"Good work," Mac said, nodding. "Bag and tag, please. Then I'd like to have them." He turned back to the door as her partner retrieved an evidence bag. "Maris, would you mind asking Ms. Sheehan to join us up here?"

Though Maris turned to go, she had a sinking feeling in her stomach. During the last couple of days, she'd seen nothing to indicate that Pammy was involved with any of the men. But Reggie's death had been upsetting and stressful for everyone, including herself. Was it possible that she'd missed something?

By the time Maris reached the living room, conversation came to a stop, and all three guests looked up at her. She turned her gaze to the artist. "Pammy, the sheriff would like a word."

"With me?" she said, almost jumping to her feet. She glanced at BJ and Felix, who looked equally surprised. "Well, I don't know what I can tell him."

Maris gave her a kind look and gestured for her to precede her. They climbed the stairs in silence, and Mac met them at the top. He had the thin black socks in a clear plastic evidence bag. Before he could question her, Pammy gaped down at the bag.

"What's that?" she asked.

"If I'm not mistaken," he said, holding them up. "They're men's black dress socks." He turned the bag so she could have a better look. "Do you recognize them?"

"Me?" she said, her voice pitched high. "Why would I recognize men's socks?"

He lowered the bag. "Because they were found in your bed."

Her head cocked back as though he'd thrown cold water in her face. She even had to sputter. "My bed?" She stared into the bedroom where the two investigators were packing up. "Are you sure?"

"I'm afraid so," Mac said. "Any idea who they might belong to? Or is it possible that you wear men's socks?"

Pammy scowled at him. "No I don't wear men's socks. Don't be ridiculous." He held them up again, but she vigorously shook her head. "I don't know where they came from, or whose they are." She looked at Maris. "They were in *my* bed?"

Maris nodded. "It's true. I was here when the team discovered them."

Pammy shook her head again, but this time hugged herself around the middle. The older investigator cleared her throat. They all had to back up a pace as the two women came through.

Mac handed the bag to the younger woman. "Thanks," he said to her, before they made their way down the stairs and left.

"They'll be examined for even the

smallest amount of organic material," he informed Pammy. "DNA will hopefully reveal to us who they belonged to." He paused and regarded her. "If they belonged to Mr. Atkinson, you might want to tell me that now. Sometimes that sort of action can sway a judge."

"A judge?" she blurted out. She looked frantically from him to Maris and back again. "They couldn't be Reggie's because he said–" She stopped suddenly, as her pale skin flushed a deep red. "Anyway," she said angrily, "they're not his."

Mac raised an eyebrow and glanced at Maris. "All right, Ms. Sheehan. I don't have any other questions for now."

"Fine," she said, not looking at either of them. "I'm going for a walk." In moments she'd stomped down the stairs and slammed the front door on her way out.

Mac pursed his lips. "What was that about? I wasn't particularly expecting anger."

Maris shook her head. "I really don't know. I haven't seen any indication that Pammy was involved with any of the men, including Reggie."

The sheriff regarded her. "Right," he finally said. "And that wasn't quite the reaction I'd have expected from someone who'd been hiding an affair." He thought for a moment then glanced down the stairs. "The guests can have access to their rooms."

"Good," Maris said, as they turned to the stairs. "I'll let them know."

"Thanks," Mac said. He checked his watch. "I think I'll visit a certain chef about a certain catered dinner."

Maris smiled at him, thinking about what Cookie had said about the fiery Frenchman. "Good luck," she said, and meant it.

19

———

By the time Mac headed to Plateau 7, Felix and BJ had decided to leave as well—though they'd headed their separate ways. With all the guests gone, Maris and Cookie decided to tackle the daily chores, particularly since the investigative team had left a bit of a mess.

As Maris made the beds that the team had rumpled, she thought about Pammy. She'd seemed genuinely shocked by the socks. But there had also been that anger in her reaction, something Mac had noticed as well. The young artist with the thick circular glasses didn't seem like a murderer, but Maris knew that meant little. Too many times she'd been shocked at what people of all types could do, particularly in a fit of passion.

Out in the hallway, she met Cookie who seemed to be finished as well.

"I don't think we need dusting and vacuuming today," Maris said, as they both went downstairs. None of the guests had spent much time at the B&B, nor were they a particularly untidy bunch.

"I agree," the chef said. "Perhaps game designers are naturally neat."

Maris smiled. "Maybe," she allowed. "But I'd hate to see an office full of empty pizza boxes."

Outside the fog had lifted, as it always did, and it looked as though the sky was perfectly clear. "It might be a nice day to spend outdoors," Cookie said. "I think I hear the herb garden calling."

"What amazing hearing you have," Maris said, laughing a little.

The chef laughed a bit too. "Herbs will do that to you." She regarded Maris. "And you?"

As they stood in the downstairs hallway, Maris considered for a moment. What she really wanted to do was get to the bottom of Reggie's murder. With no suspects to quiz or scenes to investigate further, there was only one other option. Luckily, it was an excellent one.

"I think I'm going to visit Claribel," she said. "You know, see what light the Old Girl can shed."

"Quite a bit, I imagine," Cookie said, as she headed toward the back porch with Maris following her.

Bear was working on the greenhouse and she waved at him. He paused for a moment and waved back, his motion almost too dainty, making Maris smile. As she approached the conical white tower, a light sea breeze wafted in from the bay, swirled in front of the door, and swung it ajar. As soon as Maris stepped through, it gently closed behind her.

"Good afternoon, Old Girl," Maris greeted her.

As she climbed the spiral staircase, she thought back to her first encounter with the magical being. Though it'd been a shock to find out that her aunt had been a witch and that the family had possessed a special bond with the Old Girl, Maris now marveled at how natural it felt. As the current lightkeeper, she often sought Claribel's help, and the Old

Gril never failed to give it. Maris wondered now if it wasn't something about the lighthouse being able to see so far that gave the Old Girl her unique abilities, as well as a North American record for saving sailors.

Finally at the top of the stairs, Maris stepped out onto the metal landing of the optics house and paused for a breather. "Phew!" she gasped, going to the window.

The view today was phenomenal, what she liked to call one-hundred mile visibility. Small, cottonball clouds dotted the sky in the distance, but the horizon below them was so clear that the line between ocean and sky looked as though it'd been drawn by a pencil. In the distance, a container ship with a cargo that looked like a patchwork quilt seemed to move at a glacial speed, and yet it left two lines of white waves in its wake. Little sailboats bobbed here and there, and Maris could even see the bright colors of the clothes that the boaters wore.

She held a hand against the sun to shield her eyes and took it all in. "Wow," she murmured. It was a view that never got old.

But as her breathing recovered and her pulse settled down, she turned to the heart of the lighthouse, its fresnel lens. As always the word lens amused her. If anything it was a work of art, a sculpture of crystal clear glass supported by gleaming steel. Its overall shape was that of an egg, though it was as tall as her. Most of the pieces of glass, all different shapes and sizes, were grooved with finely etched concentric circles. Maris had finally learned that these concentric grooves and the stepped arrangement of the pieces of glass were what gave the lens its name, after the French inventor.

As she watched, light bounced around inside them, fracturing into thousands of sparkles in every color imaginable. It was mesmerizing and she could watch all day, but slowly an image began to form. It was Bear working on the greenhouse.

Maris's brows drew together as she took a closer look. It was like looking through a telescope with an enlarged view. The steel structure of the greenhouse was done and Bear was starting to put in some glass.

But as suddenly as the vision had begun, it ended, simply winking out. Maris blinked.

What in the world could Bear or the

greenhouse have to do with Reggie's death? What could Claribel be trying to tell her?

She went to the window that looked down on the property. Bear was indeed in the greenhouse installing a glass panel and Cookie was in her garden, both of them working. Often the lighthouse would show her remote visions, places that she could never have seen directly even with binoculars. But this one had been close to home.

"Hmm," she muttered. Maybe she ought to go down and see what their handyman was doing.

With a smile she gently patted the base of the lens. "Thanks, Old Girl," she said quietly.

The trip down was much quicker than the trip up. When she reached Bear, he was in virtually the same place, fitting a glass panel into the side of the steel structure. Once he'd done that he bent to pick up a giant tube of caulk, but paused when he saw Maris watching him.

"Hello, Maris," he said.

"Good afternoon, Bear. I wonder if I could trouble you with a question."

He straightened up. "It's no trouble."

She paused for a moment, not quite sure

how to put this. "It may sound odd, but I was wondering if there's anything that you can tell me about Reggie Atkinson's death."

Rather than appear surprised or even mildly puzzled, the big handyman simply appeared to be thinking. "I was home by dark that day," he said. "I didn't talk to the visitors." He looked at the B&B for a moment. "I see them on the porch, but they don't come to look at what I'm doing." His gaze settled back on her. "I don't know anything about his death," he concluded. Then he shrugged, and gave her a little smile. But as he did his stomach gurgled loudly. His cheeks flushed a bright pink and he used a big hand to cover his bulging middle, but it didn't help the sound.

Maris smiled at him. "I'm going to pick up some lunch for us, so hold that thought."

He smiled sheepishly at her. "Okay." Then he turned back to the glass panel with the caulk gun.

As she strode toward the herb garden, she thought about what Claribel had shown her. It hadn't surprised her that Bear didn't know anything about the murder. But the Old Girl never showed her something without a reason. She'd have to keep it in mind.

Cookie was pulling weeds but paused and stood up as Maris approached. As she smoothed the hair out of her face with a gloved hand, she said, "Any insights?"

Maris shook her head. "I'm afraid all I learned is that it's time to get lunch."

"Not a bad thing to learn," the gardener said. "Where are you thinking of going?"

Maris glanced across the bay. Mac would be done talking to Chef Fournier by now. "I think Plateau 7 might be nice." Cookie raised an eyebrow at her but Maris grinned in return. "I'll be back in a jiffy."

20

Though the views from Plateau 7 couldn't rival those from the B&B and lighthouse, they were still magnificent. The blindingly white two-story structure was almost all glass. Situated at the edge of the rocks, the floor to ceiling windows gave the feeling that you were nearly in the bay. Small and large tables draped in immaculate white tablecloths were spaced a good distance apart, giving each a beautiful oceanfront view. On occasion, a light spray of water splashed up from the boulders below.

A dramatic glass staircase led up to the second floor, where Maris could glimpse more tables. No doubt the view there was even better. She was wondering how long the wait list was for reservations, when a Maitre

D' wearing a crisp black business suit approached her at the podium.

"Table for one?" he said. Middle-aged and trim, and perhaps a bit prim, Maris was just a little disappointed that he didn't have a French accent.

"I'd like to order take-out," she said, suddenly wondering if such an upscale restaurant even did to-go orders.

"Of course," the man said, and removed a tall black menu from behind the podium. He handed it to her. "Please, take your time," he said, before bustling off.

The lunch offerings were stupendous, capitalizing on the fresh seafood that she now knew was the chef's passion. From the lobster Thermidor to the stuffed and breaded mussels to the pan fried Sole meunière, everything looked delicious. It was impossible to decide—until she spotted the bouillabaisse. The classic fish stew was based on the Pixie Point Bay catches of the day. She caught the Maitre D's eye. As she handed him the menu, she said, "The bouillabaisse please. I'll need four servings." Like Bear himself, the handyman's appetite was outsized.

The Maitre D' bowed a little. "An excellent choice." He put the menu back and turned to head toward the nearby computer station.

"Excuse me," she said, "but I was wondering if Chef Fournier is here today?"

The man turned back to her and sniffed. "He is always here, Miss. Who can I say is inquiring?"

She smiled pleasantly. "Maris Seaver."

He nodded curtly before bringing out his phone and texting. Puzzled, she watched him send the message. "I thought the chef was here?"

The Maitre D' nodded to the kitchen door. "In the kitchen." He lowered his voice. "No one is permitted there except for the chef himself."

Maris frowned at him. That didn't make sense. A restaurant like Plateau 7 would have all kinds of sous chefs, pastry chefs, and perhaps even a saucier at work. When Chef Fournier had catered Reggie's dinner at the B&B, he'd seemed quite certain that the restaurant had been left in good hands.

Just then, Etienne Fournier, in his white chef's outfit and hat, burst from the kitchen and nearly ran to her. The Maitre D' excused himself, went to the computer station, and touched the screen.

"What is the meaning of that man coming here to ask me questions?" Fournier demanded. "Me!"

Apparently, Mac had indeed visited. She held up her hands. "I'm sure it's routine, Chef. Everyone at the B&B has been questioned too. More than once, including me and Cookie."

"It is not possible that the food is in question," he declared. "Yes, I was there. But whose house is it? Yours. Yours!"

"I agree," she said quickly. "We were searched this morning. I assume the restaurant wasn't searched?"

His eyes widened and his paper hat quivered. "Searched? No!" He lowered his voice. "That could ruin me," he whispered fiercely.

She held up her hands again. "The dinner was beyond reproach. No one doubts the food."

"I should hope not!"

She nodded. "Which is why you weren't searched." She paused to let that sink in. "In fact, the food was incredible, as you know."

"Of course it was," he agreed. "Of course." He tugged down his tunic, and took a moment to shift his hat a little. "The meal was perfection. Training tells."

Maris smiled at him. "Indeed it does. I'm sure the sheriff was only trying to see if there was something else you might have noticed. You were in a particularly good position to observe everyone during that stupendous dinner."

He seemed to be thinking as he smoothed his waxed mustache, but when he didn't reply, Maris said, "This is my first time to Plateau 7." She gazed appreciatively at the surroundings. "I must say, it lives up to its reputation."

He stood up a little straighter. "It is Plateau *Sept*, not *seven*."

"Oh," she said. "My apologies. Plateau *Sept*."

He nodded his approval and then checked left and right before leaning in closer. "I did happen to notice a little something that evening," he said lowly. "I know I can tell you since we are both...shall we say, kindred kind."

Maris nodded to him. "Exactly so."

His dark eyes twinkled. "It didn't escape my notice that the young Asian man was infatuated with the woman." The chef checked left and right again. "But she only had eyes for the boss man."

Maris's brows rose. How had she missed that? "Are you sure?"

He held up his finger. "It was only a glance or two, when they thought they were unobserved. After all," he continued, touching his chest, "it was only the server who came and went. It is often the case that the server disappears."

Maris had to nod. Even she had not kept track of Etienne as he'd served the meal. She gazed into his eyes. "Thank you."

Calmer now, he simply waved her off. "Think nothing of it." Then, as though an alarm had sounded, he said, "I will check on your food." He turned on his heel and was gone. She noticed that he stopped at one of the tables next to the window where two women were having dessert, before proceeding back to the kitchen.

Before she could even think back on the dinner, and try to remember a moment when Felix would have gazed meaningfully at

Pammy, or her at Reggie, the French chef was on his way back, carrying her order and also a silver coffee pot. He stopped at an empty table and set down the food, before pouring coffee for the two women. Then he picked up her order, and brought it to the podium. As Maris took her wallet from her purse, he simply put the large cardboard to-go box in her hands.

"With my compliments," he said gallantly.

The smell of the bouillabaisse wafted up and she could also see paper wrapped baguettes and a cucumber salad.

"Oh no," she said taking it from him. "I couldn't."

"But of course you can," the chef said. "I am afraid I must insist. You will also find menus included. Perhaps your future guests will find them of interest."

She beamed back at him. "I'll be sure to bring them to their attention. Thank you."

"Bon appétit," he said.

21

Maris dabbed the remainder of her baguette into the last little bit of soup at the bottom of her bowl. The bouillabaisse had been extraordinary. Shrimp, mussels, and crab had accompanied generous chunks of salmon and potato, all simmered to perfection in the tomato-based soup.

"I can't remember the last time I had bouillabaisse," Cookie said, sitting back in her porch chair.

Bear was just finishing as well. "Bouillabaisse," he said, as though trying the word out. He was sopping up the last of his as well. It turned out that the fish stew had been the right choice. Lunch had passed in almost complete silence.

As Maris wiped her mouth with a napkin, she remembered what Etienne had said and turned to Cookie. "I almost forgot. It turns out that Chef Fournier was being observant that night at dinner. He's of the opinion that Felix had eyes for Pammy, but that she in turn had eyes for Reggie."

Cookie frowned a bit, and cocked her head. "I must say that escaped my notice." She paused, her gaze drifting back to the house. "Then again, I was so focused on that amazing meal." She smiled at Maris. "If they'd been ogling each other and batting their eyelashes I probably wouldn't have noticed."

Maris laughed a little. "Me too. But I do recall how the chef was aware when everyone had stopped eating."

Cookie nodded. "Yes, I remember that. He was none too pleased, and rightly so. But yes, a good server is always going to be watching."

"Speaking of which," Maris said, her brow furrowing. "At the restaurant, it looked like the chef was waiting tables, and the Maitre D' said that no one was allowed in the kitchen."

Cookie blinked at her. "No one?"

"That's what he said. And when I asked to speak with the chef, the Maitre D' texted him."

Cookie's expression became guarded. "Huh," she said. "That's interesting."

"If he's that controlling," Maris asked, "how could he ever have left his restaurant to come here and cater Reggie's event?"

Cookie eyed them both, then leaned in toward them. "I don't think he did," she whispered.

Bear's bushy eyebrows went up as he tucked the last bit of bread and broth into his mouth.

Maris shook her head. "But we saw him. He served us that entire five course meal."

The diminutive chef shook her head. "I think it looked like him." She checked behind her. "But it was probably a fetch. I'll bet the waiter at the restaurant was a fetch too."

"A fetch?" Maris asked, looking from Cookie to Bear, who only shrugged his big shoulders. She looked back to Cookie. "What's a fetch?"

Cookie pursed her lips for a moment. "Think of it as a clone, a double. Maybe even a triple. Just think of how much you could get done if there were three of you." Maris sat back, staring at her. This was not a magical ability that she had ever heard of. "That has to be it," Cookie continued. "I'd bet my bottom, middle, and top dollar on it."

That might also explain why no one was allowed in the kitchen. Maris pictured an army of Etiennes moving at light speed around the stoves and ovens. She smirked a little. He was his own sous chef and saucier, and never had to worry that anything wasn't done exactly the way he wanted it.

For a few moments, the three of them sat quietly. Now Maris had to wonder if she'd spoken to the chef himself, or one of his fetches. She'd been about to ask Cookie if there was any way to tell them apart, when Bear broke the silence.

"Where do you want the door?" he asked Cookie.

"The door?" she said, sitting forward. "You're already doing the door? Ooh, let's see."

Maris stood with them and started to gather up the bowls, but Cookie put a hand on her arm. "Leave those for a minute. Let's go look at where the door should be."

Maris grinned as she set everything down. "Let's."

As they neared it, Maris could see that the glass in the roof was in place. "Bear, this is amazing." The sturdy metal supports and bracing had been painted a deep forest green. Large bolts secured it to the paving stone floor.

"Is this a louvered window?" Cookie asked, going to the back corner.

"For air flow," Bear said, stooping down to turn the small crank. The slats of glass raised up. Then he turned and went to the opposite side, reaching up to where the roof met the wall. There was another crank, which he turned, raising the hinged roof panel just above it. "It goes with this hopper window."

"That is genius!" Cookie exclaimed.

Maris stood in the middle with hands on hips. "You ought to be a builder."

The little bit of his cheeks that showed above his thick beard pinked a little. "I am building."

"So you are, my friend," Cookie said, reaching up to pat him on the shoulder. "So you are."

He smiled down at her. "The door can go

on the north side or the south." He indicated the two directions.

"Oh I think south," Cookie said. "Facing the garden." She looked at Maris. "What do you think?"

Maris nodded. "That makes sense. You'll be carrying your seedlings to and fro."

Just then a familiar toot-toot-toot sounded from the bay. All three of them turned to see Slick motor past in his fishing boat. As usual at this time of day, he was returning to the pier with his fresh catch. As one, they waved to him.

"The seedlings," Bear said as they watched Slick go past. "Do you want a table or shelves? I have some leftover wood in the truck."

"Oh," Cookie exclaimed, turning around. "Door there," she said, pointing at the garden. Then she did an about face. "Table here." She turned to Bear and clasped her hands together, beaming at him. "I can hardly wait."

"Me too," he said, smiling back at her.

"Then we'll leave you to it," she replied.

With that settled, Maris and Cookie took in the bowls and plates and started to load the dishwasher. "Once this is done," Maris said, "I'll start the laundry."

"We probably have enough towels and sheets for a week," the diminutive chef said. Although Maris held out her hand for the rinsed bowl, Cookie placed it in the dishwasher herself. "What have you done today to slow down?"

Maris knew she ought to be expecting these little check-ins by now and have an answer ready. Yet somehow she didn't. "I had a wonderful lunch and the grand tour of your future greenhouse."

As Cookie rinsed the next bowl, she gave her a stern look over her shoulder. "You know what I mean."

Maris did. Though she'd managed to finally drop a few pounds since returning to Pixie Point Bay, her cholesterol was another matter. It seemed to be the curse of the Seaver women. Add to that the Type A+ personality that they all shared, and it was the perfect combination for a cardiac arrest—something that had killed both her mother and her aunt. Maris didn't want to share the same fate, and yet she struggled with taking down time.

She sighed. "Maybe I'll grab my watercolors and do a little painting?" she said.

Cookie gave her a wink. "Now you're talking." She shooed her away. "Off with you."

But before she left, Maris grabbed the box and to-go containers from Plateau 7, but left the menus. "I'll just put this in the trash on my way."

22

———

Outside, in back of the house, Maris went to the various colored trash containers, careful to separate out the recyclables. But just as she was about to drop the cardboard box into the blue barrel, she spotted a t-shirt.

"That's not recyclable, is it?" she muttered. She consulted the plastic poster on top of the lid. Clothes were not included. "Nope, it's not."

Carefully she picked it out and took it to the black bin, but stopped before she tossed it in. It seemed in good condition, and might make a nice donation to the thrift store in Cheeseman Village—after it was washed. The charity had accepted several of her aunt's outfits as well as her lightly used shoes.

Maris took it back into the house, through to the utility room, where she tossed it onto the mound of waiting towels.

In her bedroom, she found Mojo having his daily siesta on the bed. Though she would have sworn she'd made no sound as she took her paint supplies from the desk, he raised his head and gave her a sleepy look. She gave the top of his head a gentle rub. "Back to sleep," she whispered. As though her words had drugged him, his head fell back to the comforter and his orange eyes closed.

Out on the north porch under the balcony, Maris set up two jars of water, her paper, and the pigment trays on the table. As she took a seat, she was glad to be in the shade. The afternoon sun was not only bright, but warm as well. Combined with the moisture from the bay, the air had just a tinge of sultriness to it. Maybe Mojo had the right idea with his siesta. But, as long as she was here and all set up, she might as well paint.

Though it'd been some time since she'd taken a watercolor class with local artist Clio Hearst, she'd actually stuck with the practice. As she'd been taught, she wet the thick paper with a thin sheen of water before beginning to apply the first layer of pigment.

The view down the undulating coastline was a spectacular combination of steep, buff cliffs that dropped down to meet the glittering aquamarine of the ocean. She took a bit of sienna and mixed it with some ochre and water and used broad vertical strokes for the cliffs. Purposefully preferring practice to perfection, she let her hand move quickly, watching with delight as the colors merged and spread, darkening in spots and lightening in others as the pigment flowed in the water. Satisfied with the land, she cleaned off her brush in the warm color water jar, and began to mix the blue she'd use for the ocean. But as she took a bit of ultramarine pigment on her brush, the pigment trays and everything else suddenly vanished.

Maris froze. She knew immediately that it was a flash of precognition, the magical ability that she shared with her aunt. She was just about to receive a glimpse of the future.

She saw Pammy, lounging on one of the deck chairs. But she had her knees drawn up and a sketch book resting against them. She seemed to be idly doodling, tilting her head one way and then the other. In her hand was a thin black marker and the page seemed to have some sort of large, ornate writing on it. But before Maris could make out the letters, the vision winked out.

She was staring at her paint set again, and the brush with ultramarine.

"Huh," she muttered. "Pammy." She filed the image away.

Once again she dabbed at the pigment on the mixing tray and compared it to the ocean, but it was too light. As she looked out at the bay she realized why. The sun was getting low and the water was darkening. Somehow a good chunk of the afternoon had escaped her. Although the painting was only half done, she smiled. Perhaps it was better if she let it dry before moving on to paint the water anyway. Besides, it had already accomplished its mission for the day: she'd relaxed with no sense whatsoever of time passing by.

"Nice," she said to herself as she began packing up. It was almost time to start the wine and cheese.

23

As Maris took her art supplies back to her bedroom, she passed the parlor—and had to stop. Out of the corner of her eye, she spotted Mojo perched on the Ouija board.

"What?" she quietly muttered.

Without so much as a tiny meow or scratch at the door to alert her, it looked as though he'd started on his own. Just as she stepped into the room, his paw landed on the planchette.

"Hold on," she whispered, still carrying her supplies as she hurried quietly to his side.

But the pudgy little cat took no notice of her. Instead, his glittering orange eyes seemed fixed on some faraway point beyond the confines of the room. His velvety ears cocked in every direction, spinning to and fro like small radar dishes. For all the world, he looked exactly like someone who was hearing the spirits. His fuzzy paw moved the planchette to the first letter: O.

She frowned down through the clear plastic lens. There was no one at the B&B whose name started with O. In fact, come to think of it, there was no one in Pixie Point Bay either. But as she watched, he quickly slid the heart-shaped plank to the next letter, coming to an abrupt stop over the letter I.

"O, I?" she whispered.

For a moment she wondered if he was spelling something French. Her mind flashed back to the fiery chef at Plateau 7 and a fellow magic person. But she couldn't think of any French words that started with OI—not that she knew much French to begin with. But then his paw twitched and the planchette moved a short distance before it stopped over the L.

Her brows arched upward. "Oil?"

As though uttering the word had signaled the end of the session, Mojo blinked, shook out his fur, and jumped to the floor. Without so much as a backward glance, he trotted from the room.

"Oil," she said again, staring down at the board. Like the oil in a car? Or maybe like the oil in a cruet? She thought of the lighthouse. Or maybe even like the oil in a lamp.

She shook her head and blew out a breath. There were simply too many possibilities.

Out in the hallway, she was surprised to find Mojo sitting there, cleaning his face. "Oil?" she said to him.

He looked up at her with his big orange eyes, and gave her his signature meow, and a loud one.

"Okay," she said. "I wasn't questioning your ability. You said oil. But there's a million kinds." To that he only returned to licking his paw, and then rubbed it over his forehead. "So that's it? Just oil? Are you sure you don't want to spell something else?"

In answer, he simply got up and headed toward the kitchen.

"Of course not," she muttered, watching him go. "Thanks."

24

At the dining room sideboard, Maris sliced some of the leftover Gruyere from the morning's breakfast. It's delicately flavored, slightly nutty taste would pair nicely with a light Pinot Noir. Outside the bay window, another beautiful sunset was unfolding, its dusky purple light filling the room. It looked as though she'd started preparing the Wine Down not a moment too soon.

As if to confirm that, the front door opened and closed. But rather than come down the hall, she heard heavy footsteps take the first set of stairs at the front of the house. Sometimes guests liked to freshen up or have a shower before the wine and cheese. She opened the Pinot Noir and set it near the glasses, along with the Sauvignon Blanc in its iced metal cooler. When she returned to the cheeseboard to add the final touches, the front door opened again but this time light footsteps headed to the second floor. That was probably Pammy. But then Maris heard two bedroom doors close.

"Hmm," she murmured.

But by the time the third guest returned and also promptly went to their room and shut the door, Maris had to frown down at the cheeseboard. It seemed as though the three colleagues had yet to iron out their differences, probably all of them having spent their day alone. Pammy had been extremely upset by the findings of the investigative team, but Felix and BJ apparently weren't ready to be gregarious either.

It was a shame, and not because the food was ready. Sometimes people could come together and be polite for the sake of others, like herself. In the aftermath of a death, it sometimes helped to reminisce about the departed and swap old stories. At the very least, the Wine Down really was a chance to unwind. After the stress and anxiety over Reggie's death, all of them could use at least a little of that.

But as Maris listened, there was no sound of a shower or water running in a sink. No one was freshening up. She decided to wait before opening the white wine, and poured herself a little of the local red. She'd barely had a taste, when a door slammed up above and there was the sound of raised voices. From the foot of the stairs, she heard Felix shouting.

"You sold it?" he yelled. "You sold it to Game Fame? How could you do that? It's not even yours to sell!"

"It is mine," BJ yelled back. "What I sold to Game Fame is mine. I developed that murder mystery game years ago."

"Well isn't that convenient?" Felix yelled. "You just happen to sell it right after we all work on it?"

"Wait a minute," Pammy said, her voice less angry than Felix's. "How do you know he sold Betrayal at the B&B?"

"Because I can read the internet," Felix said snidely. "Betrayal at the *Boarding House*? For pity's sake. You couldn't even think of a different name?"

"Look," BJ said, "That's my game. Reggie saw the murder mystery market heating up and resurrected an old version. But Betrayal at the Boarding House is *mine*."

"Where did you see it?" Pammy demanded.

"Where didn't I?" Felix screamed. "It's all over every forum, with his name attached. Where did you have it printed? Overseas?"

"It's none of your business," BJ shot back. "Literally."

For a moment there was silence, and then three doors slammed closed.

Maris looked down into her wine glass. There was definitely not going to be a Wine Down.

25

———

With the evening suddenly and unexpectedly to herself, Maris put away the Gruyere and Sauvignon Blanc, corked the Pinot Noir, and gathered the other leftovers. An evening of shared wine and cheese that might help the gaming trio settle their differences, or at least behave civilly, would have to wait. In the kitchen, she cleaned and stowed the cheese-board to dry, before wandering out into the hall.

Darkness had descended and Maris knew that the Old Girl's beam would be whirling around up above. Cookie had retired early, as was her usual. Quietly, Maris made her way to the end of the hall and found Mojo already waiting on the bed in her room.

"Ready to turn in early?" she asked him. In answer, he flopped to his side, stretched, and yawned, before letting his head fall to the comforter. "I see."

Maybe she'd curl up with a good book and the rest of her wine. But when she set down her glass and went back to the bedroom door to close it, her gaze fell on the hook next to it. From it hung the large black skeleton key. Most of the time as she came and went from her room, she was in a hurry and didn't see it. But tonight, it was practically glaring at her.

Maris grit her teeth. It'd been weeks since she'd made any...progress.

"Hmm," she muttered, grimacing at it.

When she'd first returned to Pixie Point Bay, she'd searched for Aunt Glenda's beautiful green pendulum after finding its conspicuously empty jewelry case in her aunt's silk boudoir box. Her gaze went up to the top of the armoire where it still rested. As she'd slowly cleared out her aunt's belongings, she'd kept it in mind and searched everything, but to no avail. With nowhere else to look but the basement, Maris had finally braved a few trips below the B&B. But of late her forays had become less about the missing green stone and more about confronting her secret: claustrophobia. The combination of a photographic memory and being trapped in a dark elevator made sure that enclosed spaces were a white-knuckle experience.

With an already sweaty hand, she slowly reached out and took the key. Little by little she'd ventured further down the basement's staircase, even dipping her head below the utility room's floor level last time. As she turned toward the utility room door at the back of her room, Mojo sat up on the bed, watching her intently.

She smiled over at him. "Care to join me?" He jumped off the bed and went to the closed door at the back, giving it a light scratch. Maris laughed a little. "Anxious, are we?"

Inside, he trotted over to the heavy wood door in the floor and sat down next to the big black lock that matched the key in her hand. But rather than draw out the anxiety and overthinking that accompanied a trip to the basement, Maris decided to change tactics. She strode quickly to the door, unlocked, and opened it. Despite her thumping heart, she was going to "walk the walk." She was going to go through the motions that a normal person would. She was simply going to pretend that the confined space didn't bother her.

Mojo flew past her and down into the darkness—making her stomach flop.

"Don't stop now," she said to herself.

As she took the steps down after him, she flicked on the light switch. The long fluorescent bulbs hummed to life and illuminated the diagonal bookcase that paralleled the stairs to the left. Rather than take a seat to investigate the beautiful collection of antique tomes, she kept walking. It was just a few more steps to the floor —and she was determined to achieve that milestone, even if she only stayed for a moment. She took the last steps with a light hop, feigning the confidence she didn't feel. As she touched bottom, she quickly glanced at the rest of the room. It was much bigger than she'd thought.

More bookcases were filled with not only books but what looked like piles of magazines. Antique trunks squatted next to wooden crates and cardboard boxes. An antique chest of drawers sat against the wall, with a well-used leather suitcase covered in faded stickers on top of it. Next to that was a tall pile of hat boxes.

The size of the room helped her to manage the welling tide of anxiety in her chest but didn't stop it. Perhaps she'd made enough progress for one day. As she turned to sprint back up the stairs, she caught a movement out of the corner of her eye. Mojo had jumped up to the top of the column of hat boxes—which was tilting.

"No," Maris exclaimed, running towards the leaning tower.

She reached it just in time, hands outstretched, but eventually had to brace it with her entire body. As she shoved them back into place with her back, Mojo leaped through the air, landing on the chest of drawers.

As she stood back and brushed the hair out of her eyes, she admonished the little cat. "You could have been hurt," she told him. Luckily the hat boxes had been light or she would never have managed it. "In fact," she said, "I'm going to make sure you don't do that again." Quickly, she unstacked the column, creating new ones only two boxes high. "There."

Again she turned to go. "Come on. We've been down here long enough."

But again, Mojo wasn't ready. Instead he leaped onto one of the new short stacks, went directly to the box that had been on top, and pawed the ribbon that tied it closed. She paused, glancing up the steps, then back at Mojo. For a moment she thought of simply grabbing him and running up the stairs. Then she had a better idea.

"Just for you," she said, taking a hold of the big round box as he leapt off. "Let's go."

As she bounded up the steps, Mojo zoomed past her. In another few moments, breathing hard and heart pounding, she closed and locked the hatch. With her back to the wall, she slowly slid down it to have a seat. She put the hat box down on the floor next to her.

"Phew," she breathed, using the back of her hand to wipe her damp brow. "Now that's what I call progress."

Mojo immediately came to her side and climbed into her lap. His big orange eyes stared up at her, and he gently rested a paw on her tummy.

She smiled down at him. "Thanks, Mojo. I'm all right." As she stroked his back, she eyed the hat box. "Shall we see what we've got?"

From the first time that she'd spotted the hat boxes, Maris had been intrigued. As far as she could recall, Aunt Glenda had never worn hats—certainly not the type that needed to be stored in a traditional box. Then again, she also hadn't known that Glenda was a witch. The box was a bit taller than it was wide, cream colored, with a burgundy top. It was held closed by a matching cream and crimson ribbon, tied in a simple bow. Gently, she took one end of the bow and tugged. As it came undone and the ribbon fell away, Mojo climbed off her lap. He gingerly touched his nose to the lid, then gave his tiny, tinny meow.

"I'm getting there," she said, putting the ribbon aside. She put her fingers under the rim of the box's top. "Here we go." She lifted it off and looked inside.

It was empty.

Maris scowled down at it, and then had to

smile. Then she had to laugh. For a second there, she actually thought she might find a witch's hat.

Mojo, however, was more intrigued than ever. He jumped inside.

"Well," Maris said to him, as he disappeared below the rim. "At least you've got a new place to play."

His head popped up, his orange eyes twinkling at her, and in his mouth, he held a toy.

"What?" she muttered, staring at him. She hadn't seen the very bottom of the box nearest her, but a toy? Two blue and white striped yarn balls were each suspended on a yarn string and tied together at the top, like a pair of cherries. "How in the world..."

Toy still in his mouth, he hopped out and took his new possession to the bedroom. Maris tilted the hat box toward her so that she could see all the way down.

Now it was empty.

She glanced toward her room, and had to smile. Yet again, Mojo seemed to have resurrected a toy that she had never seen. She looked down at the hatch door. Could the basement possibly be where he kept his stash? She shook her head. If it was, there was no hurry to find it.

Finally she got up, dusted off her backside, and picked up the empty hat box. It was time to find her glass of wine.

26

I n the morning, Maris could not only smell breakfast cooking, she could tell what it was.

"Waffles," she said to Mojo, as she opened her door and he bolted into the hallway. The sweet smell of the batter in the griddle and the prospect of maple syrup nearly made Maris want to bolt to the kitchen as well. But before she got inside, she heard the back porch door close. Someone was up early.

From the living room and through the vestibule that led to the back, Maris saw Pammy settling down in one of the chairs. She'd bundled up in a fleece jacket against the early morning fog. As Maris watched, she opened what looked like a large black art journal and then uncapped a pen.

Maris had just been about to turn away and return to the kitchen, when she remembered her brief flash of precognition. She had seen this moment yesterday. Her eyes narrowed. Somehow what Pammy was doing was important, but Maris wasn't going to be able to see anything by staying inside.

But as she exited onto the porch, she surprised Pammy, causing her to flip the journal and her pen to the porch deck.

"Oh my goodness," Maris said, "I'm so sorry. I didn't mean to startle you." The journal had landed face down, almost in front of her. She bent to pick it up.

Pammy had put a hand to her chest, but now stooped from her seat to retrieve the pen. "No worries," she said, and sat up. "I was just lost in thought."

As Maris picked up the journal and turned it over, the pages flipped by, almost to the beginning. She tried to dust if off a bit before she closed it and handed it back. "I hope it's not ruined."

Pammy scoffed a little. "Oh, it's just my morning pages. No biggie."

Maris cocked her head at the artist. "Morning pages?"

Pammy smiled up at her. "It's my morning ritual. As soon as I get up, I draw." She circled the pen in the air, next to her head. "Helps clear out the cobwebs. If something's on my mind, I get it down on paper, and then it's out. Then I can get on with other things."

"Really," Maris said. "That's fascinating. So you just draw the first thing that pops into your head?"

"Right," Pammy said. "No filter. No thinking. Just start drawing."

"Interesting," Maris said. She'd never heard of such a thing, and yet it somehow made sense. If you were trying to be creative, it might help to start with a blank slate—or at least without mental baggage.

Pammy regarded her. "Are you an artist as well as an innkeeper?"

Maris shook her head. "Oh, no. Not at all. I've taken up watercolors lately though. I find it helps me to relax."

"Ah," Pammy said nodding. "Watercolor painting. I haven't done any in years." She used the thin black pen to jot down a note on a blank page in the journal. "That's a good reminder." Then she closed it again.

A few seconds went by, and then Maris

realized that the artist was waiting for her to leave. She said, "Well, sorry again for interrupting. I've got to get back inside and see what damage I can do in the kitchen."

Pammy laughed a little. "No worries."

"See you at breakfast," Maris said, before heading back inside.

Maris went to the kitchen where she found Mojo having his usual smoked salmon breakfast and Cookie finishing with the warming trays. The crispy Belgian waffles were stacked like fallen dominoes in one tray, poached eggs were in another accompanied by a gravy boat of hollandaise sauce, and finally a tray of golden, oven-baked tater tots.

"Good morning," Maris said, picking up the first tray. "Looks like it's classics done classy today."

It never ceased to amaze her how Cookie could take the simplest of ingredients and create a breakfast buffet that rivaled those of any of the resorts where she'd worked. It didn't take a million mediocre foods to impress, just a few outstanding ones.

"Good morning," Cookie answered, in her usual cheery tone. "Sometimes it's good to get back to basics."

Once all the warming trays were in place, Maris fetched the freshly squeezed orange juice in its pretty glass pitcher, the coffee in its large carafe, and made sure the hot water dispenser did indeed have hot water. She thought about letting Pammy know that breakfast was on, but didn't want to interrupt her morning pages again. But there was no need, when she saw the artist with her journal tucked under arm enter the dining room.

"Belgian waffles," she exclaimed. "My favorite." She set the journal down on the table.

Cookie came in, took a plate, and began to heap it high with two or three of everything. Maris smiled at the diminutive chef. "Is Bear here?"

Cookie winked at her. "Just arrived. We've got to keep that young man fueled."

When Cookie was done, Maris took a plate for herself. But as she watched Pammy take a seat and slide her journal out of the way, Maris thought about when it'd fallen. When she'd picked it up, the pages had fanned by. At the time, they'd simply streamed through her vision without her actually registering what they were. But now it occurred to her that she could take her time. With Pammy's back to her, Maris discreetly reached up to her temple and tapped it. Her photographic memory did the rest.

One by one, Maris was able to stop the journal in mid page flip, and look at what had been drawn. Sketches of rooms with period furniture reminded her of the murder mystery game. That made sense. There were intricate paisleys that covered an entire page. The artist also seemed to enjoy hand lettering, in all types of styles. But near the beginning of the journal was a piece of text in a beautiful copperplate font that surprised her —particularly since it had a big "X" through it.

"Maris," Cookie said, bringing her back to the room. Maris blinked and looked over to the door. The chef's dark eyes were glittering and the woman was grinning madly. "Come

see the greenhouse," she said, and disappeared.

Maris turned to Pammy. "If you'll excuse
me," she said with mock seriousness. "I have
been summoned."

Outside, Maris could hardly believe what she was seeing. The greenhouse was finished. There was even a wood table in the back. Cookie and Bear were inside and she was nearly ricocheting around him, while he stood in the middle, holding his plate and eating. Maris entered through the new glass door.

Cookie came to a stop and beamed at her. "What do you think?"

"I think it's amazing," Maris said, her voice full of awe. "And beautiful."

All of the metal gleamed in deep forest green, and all the panes of glass had been cleaned to perfect clarity. The structure's joins and corners had received extra attention, hidden by small decorative flourishes in the shapes of dragonflies and bees. While the hopper window in the roof was cracked open just a couple of inches, the louvered window on the opposite side was fully open. Despite the foggy morning outside and the ventilation, the little glass house was very comfortable inside.

"I can't wait to start using it," Cookie crowed.

Bear shook his head a little, then quickly swallowed. "I need to finish the table."

She and Maris both eyed it. "It looks finished to me," the chef said.

It'd obviously been made from different types of wood, but it was as solid looking and nicely detailed as the surrounding structure. There was even a small shelf underneath the table top.

"I mean finish, not finish," the big man said.

Cookie looked at him "You've lost me."

"Me too," Maris added.

He went to the table and smoothed his thick fingers over it. "Raw wood without a finish," he said, looking down at it. "Without a finish, it will pick up moisture and stain."

"Oh," Cookie said. "You mean finish like a polish?"

The big man nodded and picked up a forkful of tater tots. "Furniture polish."

"Do we have any?" the chef asked.

As he chewed, he nodded.

"I've seen that sort of thing in the utility room," Maris said. "On those shelves at the end." She looked at Bear. "Will any one do?"

He shook his head. "We should have some oil of mirbane. I used it before. That would be good."

Cookie touched the table's surface. "You're going to oil it?"

Bear shook his head again. "Oil of mirbane is in polish. The polish has a different name." He held out his plate to Maris. "Could you hold this?"

"Um, sure," Maris said, exchanging a look with Cookie. As he took his phone from the deep front pocket of his bib overalls, he saw them looking at each other. "Can't put the plate on the table until it's finished."

"Ah," Maris said, as she watched Bear type in the word oil.

She went still.

Oil.

Mojo had spelled that word on the Ouija board. But as Bear spelled out "mirbane" another image popped into her mind. The big man was standing there, head bent over his phone, using it to do a search. She glanced back at the house. Then she handed the plate to Cookie. "I've got to go call the sheriff."

29

With the buffet breakfast cleared away, everyone took a seat. It was a different seating arrangement from the murder mystery dinner, but Maris couldn't help but see the parallel. Pammy and Felix sat next to each other on one side of the long table, as they had that night, while BJ and Cookie sat on the other. Maris stood at the end, near the bay windows, while the sheriff stood opposite her, near the door.

"I assume this means you've made progress," Felix said to the sheriff.

Mac nodded. He opened the manila folder that was on the table in front of him. "I have a search warrant."

"Another one?" Pammy said, a bit of a whine in her voice.

"Yes," the sheriff said. "I'd like everyone to take out their cell phones and place them on the table."

"Oh, come on," BJ said. "Our phones? We need our phones."

Mac held up the search warrant. "You'll get them back."

Maris had already known that the phones would be confiscated and brought hers with her. She laid it on the table in front of her.

As Pammy reached to her back pants pocket, Felix and BJ took their phones from their front pockets. Felix laid his on the table first. "It's new," he said, a hint of anger in his voice. "So don't damage it."

Soon everyone's cell phone was on the table—except for Cookie's. When Mac looked at her, she shrugged. "I don't own one."

Mac smiled at her and nodded then took the notepad from his breast pocket. "Passcodes?" He looked around the table. "Maris, we'll start with you. Type it into your phone as you say it out loud and show me that it works."

She quickly provided it and unlocked her phone. Pammy then did the same, but Felix said, "I don't have a security code on mine."

Pammy frowned at him. "You know that's not very safe, right?"

"BJ?" Mac asked, and BJ recited his passcode as he unlocked his phone.

"Good," the sheriff said. He set down the notepad, took out an evidence bag, and went around the table gathering up the phones. "When these are returned to you, I'd advise you to change your passcodes."

As he set the bag of phones onto the table next to the search warrant, he looked up at Maris. "Maybe you could tell us all what you've discovered."

In the silent room, all eyes turned to her.

"Of course," she said and looked around at the expectant faces. The back of her shoulders and neck tightened but she took a breath, then turned to Felix.

"After Reggie's death, when we were all in the living room," Maris said, nodding in that direction, "you told us that you'd started your own gaming company."

"That had nothing to do with his death," Felix quickly protested. "I've been working on my business plan for months. I have documentation to prove it."

"And your business loan has just been approved," Maris said, agreeing. "But I think you'd have to concur that the timing of his death was rather...fortuitous."

Felix scowled and shook his head. "I wouldn't have anything to gain from his death. I wouldn't have worked for him any more."

"Exactly," Maris said. "You wouldn't have been an employee, you'd have been a competitor."

When BJ and Pammy both looked at him, he paled. "Hey," he said, "I don't even have a damn company yet. I was going to start it on the side." He looked at them both. "It's not like I could live without a salary. I wasn't going to quit my job."

"You were going to work a full-time job *and* start a company?" BJ asked.

"That's exactly what I've been doing all these months anyway," Felix answered hotly. "I've worked my butt off just to get this far."

"You had a lot to protect," Maris said.

"That's not what I meant," he shot back, his dark eyes flashing at her.

She leveled a steady gaze at him. "The one thing we do know," Maris said calmly, "based on the reenactment, is that everyone here had the opportunity to put poison in Reggie's wine glass."

Felix glared at her, and then at Mac. "Well I didn't have any poison. I didn't kill him. I didn't *plan* on killing him, and I didn't bring any poison."

"The poison was already here in the house," Mac told him, "just like in the game."

"What?" Pammy exclaimed. "You know the poison?"

Mac looked at her. "We also know something else. We've got the DNA results from the socks found in your bed. They belonged to Reggie."

Now it was Felix and BJ's turn to stare at her. The young artist flushed a deep red. "That's ridiculous. Reggie was never even in my room. He was never–"

Maris held up a hand to her. "I believe you."

Although Pammy sputtered for a few moments, she managed to calm herself, "Well, I hope so."

"Because Reggie had rejected your advances," Maris finished.

Eyes wide, Pammy's mouth hung open as she stared at her. BJ cocked his head back, staring between Pammy and Maris, while Felix looked at the artist as though she'd grown another head.

"When the sheriff told you about the socks," Maris said to her, "you said 'They couldn't be Reggie's because he said–'" Maris paused. "Said what?"

Pammy's mouth flattened into a thin line as she glared at the table.

"When you dropped your art journal," Maris continued, "I couldn't help but see some of the drawings and calligraphy in it— particularly the early pages." Pammy looked as though she swallowed something bitter. "I saw that you had hand lettered your name along with Reggie's," Maris prompted. "Like a wedding invitation."

"Oh my god, fine," Pammy spat out. "I had a crush on the boss." She stared defiantly at Felix and then BJ as though daring them to say something. When neither of them did, she added, "But when I said something to him, he said..." She glanced at Maris. "...that he didn't feel that way about me. He just wanted us to be friends."

"That's when you drew the big X through your names," Maris said.

Pammy slowly nodded. "Right," she said quietly, her gaze drifting down to the table. Then she sat up straighter and lifted her head. "But that doesn't mean I wanted to see him dead. He didn't want me to be his girl-friend but..."

"That hadn't changed how you felt about him," Maris concluded. Pammy only nodded.

"But it wasn't for unrequited love or poaching employees that Reggie was killed." Maris turned to BJ. "It was for money." The game developer's stoney face returned her gaze. "I overheard the argument upstairs last night. You've apparently sold a game recently?"

When BJ didn't answer, Felix said, "A murder mystery game." He turned to BJ. "Betrayal at the Boarding House. I saw it on the internet."

"It must have surprised you at dinner," Maris said, "when Reggie announced he'd sold it too."

"That's right," Cookie said, speaking up

for the first time. "Some company named...Hario?"

"Exactly," Pammy agreed. "He said he'd sold it." Then she looked at BJ. "You weren't too pleased."

"He sold it to Hario," Felix said. "You sold it to Game Fame." The producer narrowed his eyes. "That was never going to work."

Finally BJ spoke up. "Having two similar but different versions of a game is nothing new," he scoffed. "Reggie and I had worked it out."

Felix scoffed in return. "It has nothing to do with what you and Reggie had 'worked out.' It's what Hario and Game Fame think when they start suing each other. Reggie would have known that. In fact, so should you."

"For the rest of the evening," Maris said, "you were on your phone." She nodded at the bag on the table. "Did you search for oil of mirbane?"

"What?" Cookie said. "Bear's finish?"

Maris nodded at her. "The very one."

BJ glanced at the phones, beads of sweat on his upper lip. "I have no idea what you're talking about."

Maris smiled at him. "Then let me explain it. Oil of mirbane is another way of saying nitrobenzene. It's a common part of polishes and household cleaners—and it's highly toxic. Absolutely deadly. Is that what your internet searches revealed? It must have seemed like a dream come true when you learned that nitrobenzene smells of almonds and tastes sweet."

"Reggie got drunk so fast," Pammy whispered, eyes wide.

"This is ridiculous," BJ declared, unable to keep from glancing at the phones. "If I searched for poisons while we play tested, it only makes sense. That's what the whole mystery was about."

"We'll be pulling the entire search history," Mac told him. "I wonder if you might have been curious about time of death, or signs of poisoning."

"The next morning," Maris said, "you were the last one down. Is that when you took Reggie's socks and put them in Pammy's bed?"

"You people are insane." BJ shook his head and pushed back from the table. "But more to the point, this is all just coffee house conjecture." He stood up. "You don't have a single thread of hard evidence that connects anyone with Reggie's death, let alone me."

"Mr. Ridder," Mac said, shifting his stance. "Please have a seat. We're not done."

Although the game developer looked as though he might make a dash for it, he slowly sat back down. Mac nodded to Maris.

"There's just one more thing," she said. "It didn't seem like anything at the time, except maybe the wrong thing in the wrong trash bin." She looked at them all. "I was taking out the recyclables and found a t-shirt in the blue bin."

"Clothes aren't recyclable," Cookie said.

"No," Maris agreed. "They're not. So I picked it out. It looked in good shape so I thought I could wash it and donate it to the thrift store in Cheeseman Village." She smiled at the chef. "But, as instructed, I didn't do the laundry that day. I did some painting instead. I never did wash it."

Mac took a step toward BJ. "Forensics has confirmed that it has traces of nitrobenzene. DNA will take another day." He looked pointedly at BJ. "We'll be comparing it to yours."

Though BJ stood, he made no move to leave. "I want a lawyer."

Mac removed the handcuffs from his utility belt. "I think that'd be advisable, Mr. Ridder. Please put your hands behind your back. You're under arrest for the murder of Reggie Atkinson."

30

As Maris took another pot of herbs into the greenhouse, Bear set down the big bag of potting soil next to the table.

"Rosemary," Cookie said, as she took the pot from Maris and put it on the gleaming table with the others. She slid her fingers along the smooth surface. "It's hard to imagine that something that makes a piece of furniture so pretty could also kill someone."

Bear straightened up. "Always use gloves with polish and cleaners. Always."

All three of them headed back to the garden for the rest of the pots. "How did you make the connection?" Cookie asked.

"It was Bear," Maris said, picking up a pot.

He paused, one bunch of potted herbs in each hand. "Me?"

Maris nodded. "When you took out your phone," she said, as Cookie handed her another planting. "It reminded me of BJ and how he'd been looking at his phone all evening." As they headed back to the greenhouse, Maris added, "And Mojo, of course."

"Aha," Cookie said, grinning. "And what did our feline medium channel for you?"

Maris glanced to the B&B and saw him watching them from Cookie's bedroom window. She gave him a little wave, and saw him meow.

"On the Ouija board, he spelled the word oil." In the greenhouse, Cookie and Bear stared at her. "I kid you not."

As they placed the last herbs in place, Maris indicated the lighthouse. "The Old Girl showed me this greenhouse. So I knew that it would have something to do with the murder."

"The oil of mirbane again," Bear said.

"Exactly," Maris said, dusting off her hands. "It was the tarot clue that I finally had to give up on. I had to do a few internet searches."

"Tarot clue?" Cookie said, arranging the pots into rows.

"Mojo had picked the Knight of Cups."

"Cups for the poison?" Bear asked.

"That's what I thought," Maris said. "But when I did a search for Barney Jaeger Ridder, I recalled that he'd said his name was Danish. I then discovered that his last name in Danish means knight."

"Wow," Cookie said, as they all looked back at the B&B, but Mojo was no longer in the window.

In the late morning sun the Victorian greenhouse was getting warm. Bear lifted the hopper window and propped it open for a breath of sea air. "Everything is done?" he asked.

Whether he meant the greenhouse or the murder, Maris wasn't sure. But Cookie said, "Yes. Pammy and Felix have checked out and were headed to the sheriff's station for their phones. So it's time to wash all the laundry and get the rooms ready for the next guests."

But as the chef turned to go, Maris put a hand on her arm. "Not so fast." She gazed out at the herb garden and then at the aromatic pots on the table, before she smiled at her companions. "Perhaps we can just take a moment. You know, slow down for a bit. Just enjoy what we have here."

Cookie grinned and winked at her, before she closed her eyes and took in a deep breath, slowly letting it go. Bear tilted his head from side to side, cracking his neck, before he stood tall and put his palms against the ceiling, stretching. Maris bent over a pot of rosemary and inhaled its fresh and slightly pine-like scent. By the time she straightened, she found Cookie and Bear smiling at her. On impulse, she pulled them into a group hug.

The chef immediately hugged her close and, although Bear stiffened at first, his big arms eventually settled around their shoulders.

"I'm glad to be here with you guys," Maris said.

"Ditto," Cookie answered.

"Me too," said the big man, just as someone's stomach gurgled.

With the three of them standing so close, it was impossible to tell who was hungry, but all three of them backed up and simultaneously held their stomachs. As Maris and

Cookie burst into laughter, Bear quietly chuckled.

"Show of hands for who wants lunch?" Maris said, as she raised her hand, followed quickly by Bear and Cookie. "Good," she said grinning. "I'll pick up sandwiches in town."

As Maris headed back to the house, she paused for a moment and looked back. Bear was moving another bag of potting soil into the greenhouse, and Cookie was looking through her packets of seed. Beyond them the bay glittered with sapphire tones under the blazing yellow circle of the sun. Maris smiled as she turned away, already looking forward to coming back.

Another Pixie Point Bay book awaits you in The Witch Who Tasted Murder (Pixie Point Bay Book 5).

For a sneak peek, turn the page.

SNEAK PEEK

The Witch Who Tasted Murder

Excerpt

CHAPTER ONE

If only Maris Seaver's guests knew what she had to endure for the sake of wine. It was too warm; it was crowded; and it was loud. Somehow the idyllic scene she'd envisioned for the fall harvest of Alegra Winery's Zinfandel crop had not included heavy machinery. Her companion, Rosamel Alegra, had to raise her voice to be heard above the din.

"These were on the vine not thirty minutes ago," the young woman said, pointing to one of the many large plastic containers. It was heaped high and overflowing with long bunches of dusky purple grapes.

Maris guessed that Rosamel was in her late twenties. Olive skinned and short, she wore her long and tightly curled hair in a dark cascade around her shoulders and down her back.

Where she was pointing, a forklift raised the container up some twenty feet in the air, then rolled over to park next to a machine that looked like an enormous cigar. It had to be ten feet long, with a V-shaped hopper at the top. As they watched, the operator rotated the full container in midair, tipping its juicy contents into the big metal V. Hundreds of bunches of grapes, along with some leaves and stems, fell into the machine. Although some of the fruit managed to escape by clinging to the container before falling to the floor, no one paused to pick it up. The forklift was already backing away for the next batch. The pace was almost manic.

Rosamel leaned in and put her mouth near Maris's ear. "That's the crusher," she said.

A couple of men in rubber aprons and boots quickly adjusted the location of the enormous metal pan underneath it. Though the aroma of freshly picked fruit was thick, the wide waterfall of juice that now splashed into the pan filled the air with a new scent that was sweet and spicy at the same time.

"Amazing," Maris said, almost shouting. "From the vineyard to juice in under an hour."

Rosamel nodded. "Let's step outside." She pointed to the front of the cement room and headed that way.

Maris followed her through the cavernous opening into the dirt yard just beyond. Outside, the vineyard proper was only yards away. Acres upon acres of vines spread out in every direction. On what had to be one of the last warm days of the season, the sun blazed down from a powder blue sky to the heated soil.

As she and Rosamel neared the immaculate rows of plants, the young woman came to a stop and turned back to the winery. The bustle of the harvest was finally far enough away to talk.

"We do the sorting out here," she said, pointing to a conveyor belt.

A half-dozen men and women stood on

either side of it, hands and arms flying, picking out mostly twigs and clumps of leaves, but also the occasional cluster of grapes. They simply tossed the unwanted material to the ground. The fruit that made it through sorting was dumped by the conveyor belt into one of the large containers at the end. On the other end of the belt, a small tractor brought over a long cart full of stacked crates. As Maris watched, the forklift went to work again, lifting each crate and dumping it on the moving belt.

"It's not what you thought," Rosamel said. "Is it."

Maris had to laugh. "Not quite." Images of plump peasants in bare feet who were happily stomping grapes in giant wooden vats would have to be banished.

"It's a business," the young woman said.

"And quite a successful one," Maris observed, "judging by the number of employees." There had to be twenty or thirty people sorting and crushing. She gazed out to the rolling vineyard with its lush green plants as far as the eye could see. Who knows how many more people were in the fields?

Now it was Rosamel's turn to laugh. "A lot of these wonderful folks are volunteers."

Maris frowned and looked at her, and then at the sorters. They were sweaty and filthy and working a mile a minute. "You're kidding."

Rosamel shook her head, smiling. "Nope. It's a time-honored tradition. We'll be feeding them and I can guarantee you that the wine will flow." She nodded toward the conveyor belt. "We've got volunteers who've been with us for ten years running." The young woman crooked up one dark eyebrow. "It helps when you win awards."

"Ah," Maris said, nodding. In essence, that was also why she was here. Alegra Winery had been producing gold medal winners since their first release ten years ago. She had made them a staple at the B&B, her go-to wine, which was the reason for her visit today. She bought by the case. "It would seem that nothing succeeds like success."

Yet something about Rosamel and the winery's amazing achievements felt like more than know-how and elbow grease. If Maris wasn't mistaken, something a bit magical might be at work as well.

Rosamel lowered her voice. "We even have a buyer for this year's releases."

Maris regarded her. "A buyer?"

The young woman nodded, her mass of dark curls bobbing. "He wants the entire release."

Maris stared at her. "Wait. Are you saying he wants to buy everything?" She glanced at the conveyor belt and all the containers waiting to be poured onto it. "And it has yet to be made into wine?"

Rosamel grinned at her. "You've got it."

"Every varietal?" Maris asked, still trying to wrap her head around a purchase of that size. She gestured to the scene in front of them and then the surrounding vines.

"The entire release," Rosamel confirmed.

Maris's eyebrows rose as she went through the numbers in her head. Hundreds, maybe thousands, of bottles of wine that were yet to be made were already spoken for. It had to be hundreds of thousands of dollars worth of wine.

"A single buyer wants it all?" Maris asked, still a bit incredulous. "Even if you drink a bottle every..."

Rosamel shook her head quickly. "Oh no.

I'm sure he'll sample it, of course. But it's an investment. He'll sit on it for...who knows how long." She lifted her shoulders and hands. "Ten years? Twenty? Fifty?" She crossed her arms over her chest, watching the volunteers sorting. Another giant container of grapes was dumped on the belt. "He'll let go of a few cases here, a few cases there, a few at auction."

"Wow," Maris said. It was like buying artwork, or maybe stocks.

"It's an investment," Rosamel said again, "and a smart one, even if I do say so myself." She gave Maris a little elbow. "But don't worry. I'm going to set aside your usual purchase at your usual price. The deal hasn't been cinched yet."

Maris's eyes widened. "*Thank you*. I appreciate that."

The young woman nodded to her. "You're very welcome. We local folk gotta stick together." She glanced back to the winery. "Speaking of which, shall we go back to the tasting room? I'm sure today's purchase will be ready by now."

As they headed back toward the crushing room, Maris said, "Thank you very much for the tour as well—especially at this busy time of year. It's been incredibly interesting."

Rosamel waved a hand. "My busy time is over, thank goodness. Now that the harvest is almost all in, it's up to my father to make the wine. He's the one who'll–"

Despite the cacophony of the machinery, loud voices rose above it. When Maris looked over, a young man at the crusher was being grabbed from behind by an older man, who had him by the collar.

"Oh no," Rosamel muttered, heading in their direction.

· · · · ·

Buy The Witch Who Tasted Murder

FREE BOOK

If you'd like to learn how Maris arrived in Pixie Point Bay and got her start, you can read *The Witch Who Saw the Light* for FREE by signing up for my newsletter at the link below.

Get A Free Book

DEDICATION

For Mr. Bee's Knees

COPYRIGHT

Copyright © 2020 Emma Belmont

This is a work of fiction. Names, characters, places, and incidents are products of the author's imagination or are used fictitiously and are not to be construed as real. Any resemblance to actual events, locales, organizations, or persons, living or dead, is coincidental.

All rights reserved. No part of this book may be used or reproduced in any manner, stored in or introduced into a retrieval system, or transmitted, in any form, or by any means (electronic, mechanical, photocopying, recording, or otherwise), without the prior written consent of the copyright owner.

The scanning, uploading, and distribution of this book via the Internet or via any other means without the permission of the copyright owner is illegal. Please purchase only authorized electronic editions, and do not participate in or encourage electronic piracy of copyrighted materials. Your support of the author's rights is appreciated.

www.ingramcontent.com/pod-product-compliance
Lightning Source LLC
Chambersburg PA
CBHW050516190726
48284CB00003B/826